MARION COUNTY PUBLIC LIBRARY
321 MONROE STREET
FAIRMONT, WV 2655

DANGEROUS REPTILIAN CREATURES

The Encyclopedia of Danger

DANGEROUS ENVIRONMENTS

DANGEROUS FLORA

DANGEROUS INSECTS

DANGEROUS MAMMALS

DANGEROUS NATURAL PHENOMENA

DANGEROUS PLANTS AND MUSHROOMS

DANGEROUS PROFESSIONS

DANGEROUS REPTILIAN CREATURES

DANGEROUS SPORTS

DANGEROUS WATER CREATURES

CHELSEA HOUSE PUBLISHERS

The Encyclopedia of Danger

DANGEROUS REPTILIAN CREATURES

Missy Allen
Michel Peissel

CHELSEA HOUSE PUBLISHERS
New York   Philadelphia

THE ENCYCLOPEDIA OF DANGER includes general information on treatment and prevention of injuries and illnesses. The publisher advises the reader to seek the advice of medical professionals and not to use these volumes as a first-aid manual.

On the cover   Watercolor painting of a Russell's Viper by Michel Peissel.

Chelsea House Publishers

Editor-in-Chief   Richard S. Papale
Managing Editor   Karyn Gullen Browne
Copy Chief   Philip Koslow
Picture Editor   Adrian G. Allen
Art Director   Nora Wertz
Manufacturing Director   Gerald Levine
Systems Manager   Lindsey Ottman

The Encyclopedia of Danger
Editor   Karyn Gullen Browne

73-73660mm

Staff for DANGEROUS REPTILIAN CREATURES
Associate Editor   Jake Goldberg
Copy Editor   Danielle Janusz
Production Editor   Marie Claire Cebrián-Ume
Editorial Assistant   Laura Petermann
Designer   Diana Blume

Copyright © 1993 by Chelsea House Publishers, a division of Main Line Book Co. All rights reserved.

Printed in Mexico.

First Printing

1 3 5 7 9 8 6 4 2

Library of Congress Cataloging-in-Publication Data

Peissel, Michel
Dangerous reptilian creatures/Michel Peissel, Missy Allen.
p. cm.—(The Encyclopedia of danger)
Includes bibliographical references and index.
Summary: Introduces dangerous reptiles found in the world, from the black mamba to the tiger snake.
ISBN   0-7910-1789-3
        0-7910-1934-9 (pbk)
1. Dangerous reptiles—Juvenile literature. [1. Reptiles. 2. Dangerous animals.]
I. Allen, Missy. II. Title. III. Series: Peissel, Michel, Encyclopedia of danger.

QL645.7.P45 1992
597.9'0465—dc20

91-46640
CIP
AC

CONTENTS

The Encyclopedia of Danger   6
Dangerous Reptilian Creatures   9
- Black Mamba   14
- Blood Flukes   18
- Boomslang   22
- Bushmaster   26
- Cobra   30
- Copperhead   36
- Coral Snake   40
- Cottonmouth   44
- Crocodiles and Alligators   48
- Diamondback Rattlesnake   52
- Fer-de-lance   56
- Gaboon Viper   60
- Gila Monster   64
- Guinea Worm   68
- Habu   72
- Komodo Dragon   76
- Krait   80
- Land Leech   84
- Neotropical Toad   88
- Poison Frogs   92
- Reticulated Python   96
- Rough-skinned Newt   100
- Russell's Viper   104
- Taipan   108
- Tiger Snake   112

Appendix I: Snakebites   116
Appendix II: Bites, Gorings, Maulings, and Shock   121
Further Reading   124
Index   125

THE ENCYCLOPEDIA OF DANGER

"Mother Nature" is not always motherly; often she behaves more like a wicked aunt than a nurturing parent. She can be unpredictable and mischievous—she can also be downright dangerous.

The word *danger* comes from the Latin *dominium*—"the right of ownership"—and Mother Nature guards her domain jealously indeed, using an ingenious array of weapons to punish trespassers. These weapons have been honed to a fatal perfection during millions of years of evolution, and they can be insidious or overwhelming, subtle or brutal. There are insects that spray toxic chemicals and insects that go on the march in armies a million strong; there are snakes that spit venom and snakes that smother the life from their victims; there are fish that inflict electric shocks and fish that can strip a victim to the bones; there are even trees that exude poisonous gases and flowers that give off a sweet—and murderous—perfume.

Many citizens of the modern, urban, or suburban world have lost touch with Mother Nature. This loss of contact is dangerous in itself; to ignore her is to invite her wrath. Every year, hundreds of children unknowingly provoke her anger by eating poisonous berries or sucking deadly leaves or roots; others foolishly cuddle toxic toads or step on venomous sea creatures. Naive travelers expose themselves to a host of unsuspected natural dangers, but you do not have to fly to a faraway country to encounter one of Mother Nature's sentinels; many of them can be found in your own apartment or backyard.

The various dangers featured in these pages range from the domestic to the exotic. They can be found throughout the world, from the deserts to the polar regions, from lakes and rivers to the depths of the oceans,

The Encyclopedia of Danger

from subterranean passages to high mountaintops, from rain forests to backyards, from barns to bathrooms. Which of these dangers is the most dangerous? We have prepared a short list of 10 of the most formidable weapons in Mother Nature's arsenal:

Grizzly bear. Undoubtedly one of the most ferocious creatures on the planet, the grizzly needs little provocation to attack, maul, and maybe even eat a person. (There is something intrinsically more terrifying about an animal that will not only kill you but eat you—and not necessarily in that order—as well.) Incredibly strong, a grizzly can behead a moose with one swipe of its paw. Imagine what it could do to *you*.

Cape buffalo. Considered by many big-game hunters to be the most evil tempered animal in all of Africa, Cape buffalo bulls have been known to toss a gored body—perhaps the body of an unsuccessful big-game hunter—around from one pair of horns to another.

Weever fish. The weever fish can inflict a sting so agonizing that victims stung on the finger have been known to cut off the finger in a desperate attempt to relieve the pain.

Estuarine crocodile. This vile human eater kills and devours an estimated 2,000 people annually.

Great white shark. The infamous great white is a true sea monster. Survivors of great white shark attacks—and survivors are rare—usually face major surgery, for the great white's massive jaws inflict catastrophic wounds.

Army ants. Called the "Genghis Khans of the insect world" by one entomologist, army ants can pick an elephant clean in a few days and routinely cause the evacuation of entire villages in Africa and South America.

Blue-ringed octopus. This tentacled sea creature is often guilty of over-kill; it frequently injects into the wound of a single human victim enough venom to kill 10 people.

The Encyclopedia of Danger

Black widow spider. The female black widow, prowler of crawl spaces and outhouses, produces a venom that is 15 times as potent as rattlesnake poison.

Lorchel mushroom. Never make a soup from these mushrooms—simply inhaling the fumes would kill you.

Scorpion. Beware the sting of this nasty little arachnid, for in Mexico it kills 10 people for every 1 killed by poisonous snakes.

DANGEROUS REPTILIAN CREATURES

Reptiles are everywhere. Antarctica is the only continent not reputed to have a reptile whose bite is fatal, and only Iceland, Ireland, and New Zealand have no snakes at all. It is often stated that people have a natural dislike of reptiles, and in Western mythology the devil is first seen as a serpent. But one should not malign one's ancestors. We mammals are the direct descendants of the reptiles, so perhaps we should try to come to terms with them.

About 150 million years after amphibians began crawling over the earth, the reptiles evolved and freed themselves from the need for an aquatic environment. This new freedom was made possible by the development of a new type of egg that had a hard protective shell and could be laid on land. A second internal membrane protected the embryo, and the yolk nourished it until the egg hatched. From an evolutionary point of view, reptiles now stand between semiaquatic amphibians and the more advanced birds and mammals.

Reptiles make up the class Reptilia and are air-breathing vertebrates that are covered with scutes, or horny scales. This tough outer covering protects reptiles from loss of body moisture. There are about 5,000 species of turtles, lizards, snakes, and crocodiles. Because they are cold-blooded and depend on their environment for warmth, they are found mostly in tropical and temperate climates.

The first reptiles were medium-sized animals, about two to five feet in length, that looked like salamanders or cumbersome lizards. Today's reptiles have three-chambered hearts and muscular and skeletal

Dangerous Reptilian Creatures

modifications that allow the eyes a lateral view. The structure of their skulls provides room for stronger and more complex jaw muscles. Locomotion is achieved in various ways: a primitive walk like that of the crocodile; a longer-legged running step like that of the smaller and more agile lizards; a walking-paddling-rowing movement like that of land and sea turtles; or the sinuous undulations of worm lizards and snakes.

The senses of sight, hearing, touch, and smell are common to all reptiles, but several lizards and snakes have extra, specialized sensory organs. The ability to detect heat is common. Reptiles also vary greatly in their feeding habits. Some are strict vegetarians, and others are strict carnivores (meat eaters). Still others are omnivorous, eating both meat and plant matter.

Except when hunting, the reptile's most common defensive move is to attempt escape, and it will only bite when threatened or cornered. Most attacks on humans are the result of foolish actions by the victims.

The metabolic rate of a cold-blooded reptile is only about 10 percent of that of a warm-blooded bird or mammal; thus they require much less food. A 12-foot crocodile does not eat as much as a small penguin. If food is scarce, a reptile will just return to its burrow and wait until things improve. Most reptiles mate once a year, and as with most mammals, the male is the pursuer, and the female is relatively passive. Courtship rituals vary greatly.

Living reptiles are roughly grouped into three branches: crocodiles, which are actually closely related to birds; turtles, which are only distantly related to other living reptiles; and snakes. Inasmuch as 16 venomous snakes will be discussed in this volume, perhaps we should give them a closer look.

Every year, over 50,000 people are bitten by snakes in the United States alone. Most fatalities are children, the elderly, or members of religious sects who handle venomous serpents. Rattlesnakes account for 70 percent of venomous snakebites and almost all deaths in the United States. A snake's venom apparatus consists of glands, ducts, and one or more fangs located on either side of the head. The size of the gland

Dangerous Reptilian Creatures

depends on the size and species of the snake. During envenomization the muscles around the gland contract, forcing the venom through the ducts and then discharging it through the fangs. Envenomization only occurs in about 20 percent to 50 percent of venomous snakebites, and snakes rarely eject the full contents of their glands. Venom is essentially composed of digestive enzymes, which are necessary for an animal whose teeth are too fine to tear or crush food. When a snake envenomates, it injects a substance that breaks down living tissues and starts the digestive process even before the snake's prey is dead.

Except for the mambas, all these creatures strike only when feeding or in self-defense. Their fangs and venom are not really designed for attacking large animals such as human beings. Left alone, most reptiles are not out to harm us. Avoid playing with or threatening such animals, and they will try to avoid you.

KEY

HABITAT

FOREST

SEA

WOOD/TRASH

TOWNS

SHORE

GRASS/FIELDS

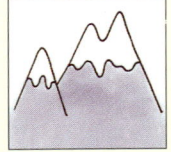
MOUNTAINS

SWAMP/MARSH

GARDEN

FRESH WATER

JUNGLE

BUILDING

DESERT

CITIES

KEY

HOW IT GETS PEOPLE

 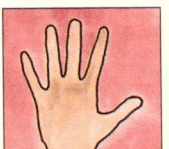  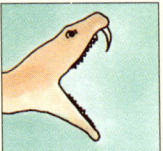

INGESTION TOUCH STING BITE

 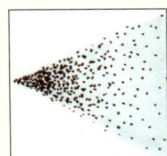 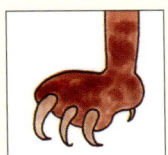

SPIT SPRAY MAUL

CLIMATIC ZONE

TEMPERATE TROPICAL ARCTIC

MORTALITY

ONE TWO THREE FOUR

BLACK MAMBA

HOW IT GETS PEOPLE

Dendroaspis polylepis

HABITAT

CLIMATIC ZONE

RATING

Black mamba? No, it has nothing to do with that lively, syncopated Cuban beat. The black mamba, because of its large size, speed, extremely toxic venom, ability to strike at great distances, and extreme agressiveness, is the most feared snake in Africa. The black mamba is such a terror that bus drivers traveling through its territory stop in fear when they see one of these giant snakes cross the road in front of them. They are especially loathed by the Zulu herders of Natal in southern Africa, where they kill great numbers of cattle by biting them on the head—no, not the hoof, the head! Able to keep their heads 20 inches off the ground as they move, they can strike at extraordinary heights. And they move fast. Clocked at seven miles per hour, the black mamba is the fastest snake in the world. It moves through trees just as swiftly as it slithers through long grass and thick ground cover.

Black Mamba

Forget the idea that a dead mamba is a good mamba. In West Africa, a native put in his pocket the head of a black mamba that he had just shot, to use as a fortifier in a tribal remedy. A short while later he encountered some friends and took the head out to show it to them. He was promptly, though not fatally, bitten.

The mortality rate for black mamba bites is exceedingly high. In one highly reputed scientific study in Natal the mortality rate was 100 percent. No wonder so many Africans are terrified. The American naturalist Roger A. Caras recounts a story about a young friend of his who was walking with a companion and encountered a black mamba at least 12 feet long. "It displayed after its fashion and the two boys froze. They had had experience with mambas before. After satisfying itself that it had been suitably terrifying, the snake slithered down from the bush where it had been when encountered and crawled across the feet of the boy nearest to it and between the legs of the other. It did not offer to strike either. They stood absolutely paralyzed and when they finally turned their heads to be certain the coast was clear they saw that the snake had ascended another bush about ten feet away and was watching them

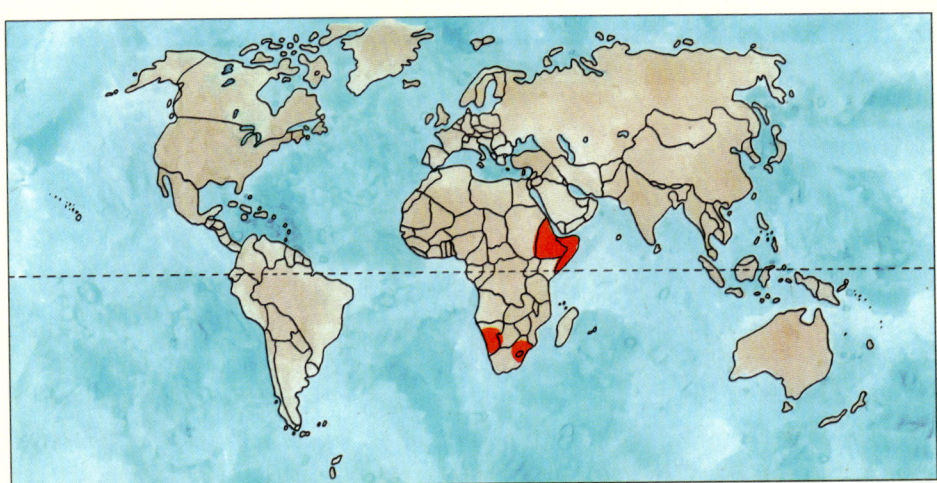

Dangerous Reptilian Creatures

very intently. The movement they made with their heads prompted the snake to do its threat display a second time. Only after several more minutes did the nervous mamba move away. There is no way of describing the condition of the nerves of the two teenagers."

Name/Description
The black mamba (*Dendroaspis polylepis*) is the largest venomous snake in Africa, sometimes over 14 feet in length, and the second largest snake in the world. It is not black, but olive-brown or gray-brown. Characterized by rapid, agile, and elegant movements, this member of the family Elapidae is highly aggressive. Its smooth scales are arranged in diagonal rows. The lower teeth are quite large, and the poisonous fangs are located in the upper jaw. Basically arboreal, meaning that it prefers to live in the trees, the black mamba feeds on birds, lizards, and frogs.

When alarmed, black mambas raise their necks and open their mouths in a threatening pose. They strike rapidly and repeatedly in a series of lightning-quick bites.

Toxicology
Black mamba venom inhibits breathing and attacks the nerves that regulate the heart. In low concentrations, the venom acts as an anticoagulant, thinning the blood, and in high concentrations, it acts as a coagulant, clotting the blood. This plays havoc with the circulatory system. But death from respiratory failure usually occurs before the victim goes into circulatory shock. The principal toxic compounds in the venom are cholinesterase, L-amino-acid oxidase, ophio-adenosine, triphosphate, and other substances.

Symptoms
Dendroaspis envenomization is noted for the speed at which the symptoms develop. Though there is almost no initial pain or swelling, there

Black Mamba

The bite of a black mamba snake can kill a person in just 20 minutes.

is profuse salivation and some dizziness, followed by restlessness and psychological disturbance. There will then be acute difficulty in breathing, followed by a drop in blood pressure, and coma, before death occurs from respiratory failure.

Treatment and Prevention

See Snakebites, page 116. An antivenin for *Dendroaspis* is available in South Africa.

BLOOD FLUKES

Genus Schistosoma

 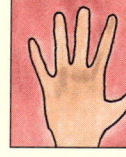   

| HOW IT GETS PEOPLE | HOW IT GETS PEOPLE | HABITAT | CLIMATIC ZONE | RATING |

If you choose to dangle your toes in the cool waters of the oasis of El Mamoun or trail your hand behind a felucca on the Nile, you may discover that these placid waters conceal a hidden danger. Bilharzia, also known as schistosomiasis, is not as deadly as some other tropical diseases, but it is nonetheless a debilitating and sometimes fatal disease caused by blood flukes, a class of tiny parasitic flatworms. These microscopic worms can burrow through any area of exposed skin and do not need to find an open cut or body opening to infect their host. Common points of infection are the urinary tract and the genital area, which become inflamed and scarred.

Blood flukes spend part of their intricate life cycle inside a species of freshwater snail so tiny that a dozen could easily fit into a teaspoon. Stimulated by the bright sunshine and higher water temperatures of the day, blood flukes abandon the snails for human hosts, who are usually agricultural workers wading barefoot in irrigation canals or women washing clothing by the riverside. The worms may remain undetected for years, spreading through the liver, stomach, and intestines, laying eggs that escape the body, hatch in the water, and give rise to a new generation of worms that reinfect the river's snails.

Blood Flukes

In large areas along the Nile in Egypt, up to 90 percent of the population is infected with bilharzia. One of its least attractive symptoms is blood in the urine. When Napoléon marched into Egypt, he encountered such widespread infection that he referred to Egypt as "the land of menstruating men." The disease has been known since the time of the pharaohs and is mentioned in papyrus writings dating back to 1500 B.C. Fossilized worm eggs found in two mummies of the 20th dynasty substantiate this. Bilharzia was also known to the ancient civilizations of China and Mesopotamia. Worldwide, schistosomiasis affects more than 225 million people, making it the second most common disease in the world after malaria.

Even if you do not go near a river or canal, you can still catch bilharzia by eating food or drinking water contaminated with blood flukes. If contaminated water is kept standing for a few days before it is consumed, the flukes will die without a host to infect, so stale water is usually safe to drink. Just beware of fresh water. In some areas bilharzia is so prevalent that people traveling overland by Jeep are advised to carry rubber gloves in case they have to dip their hands in fresh water to refill the vehicles' radiators!

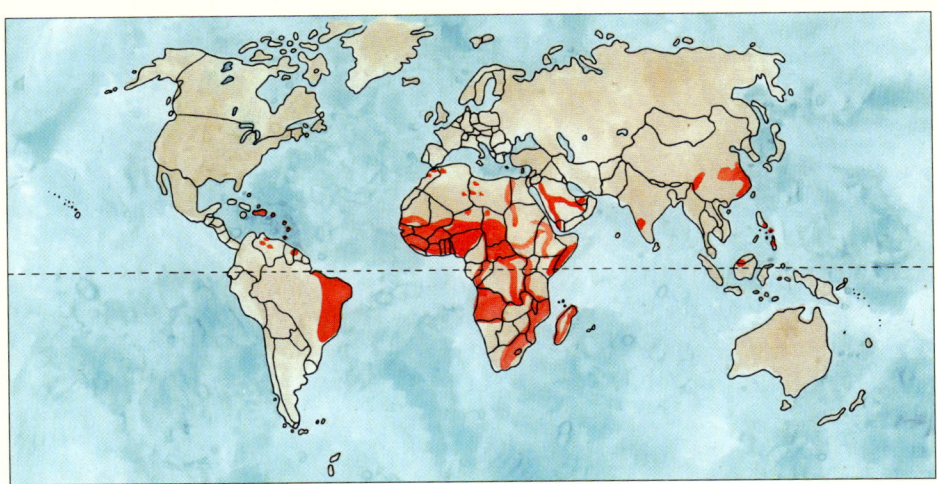

Dangerous Reptilian Creatures

Name/Description
Named in 1852 for its discoverer, Theodor Bilharz, bilharzia is also known as *fièvre de safari* (safari fever) and snail fever. Blood flukes comprise six species of schistosomes, members of the Trematoda class of flatworms. These parasitic worms are usually leaf shaped and resemble small, flat fish. Trematodes are grayish white in color and measure about one inch long. They have two suction discs for holding on to their host while feeding. Their complex life cycle depends specifically on the presence of freshwater snails and human beings. (Infected snails release large numbers of minute, free-swimming larvae, called cercariae, that are capable of penetrating unbroken skin anywhere on a human host. The larvae must locate a host within 48 hours after they are released in order to survive.) After penetration, the worms travel to the host's lungs and liver, where they mature and mate, settling in blood vessels surrounding the bladder and adjacent organs.

Infection
Blood flukes enter the body through contaminated food or drinking water, or through the skin, urethra, or rectum of persons swimming in contaminated water. Once inside the body, they feed on blood or on nutrients in the host's digestive system. The harmful symptoms of the disease are caused by the fluke's eggs, which produce bleeding, ulceration, and the formation of small growths as they penetrate body tissues.

Symptoms
Symptoms may take months to develop and vary with the species, but the victim usually develops an itchy, localized rash that disappears in a day or two, followed by a symptomless period lasting from four to six weeks. Later symptoms include fatigue and lethargy, loss of appetite, night sweats, a new rash resembling hives, and a late-afternoon fever. Blood may then appear in the urine, and urination may be frequent and painful. Bloody diarrhea and fibrosis of the liver follow. If the disease continues its course without treatment, kidney function may be impaired, and cystitis, or inflammation of the urinary tract, may occur. This

Blood Flukes

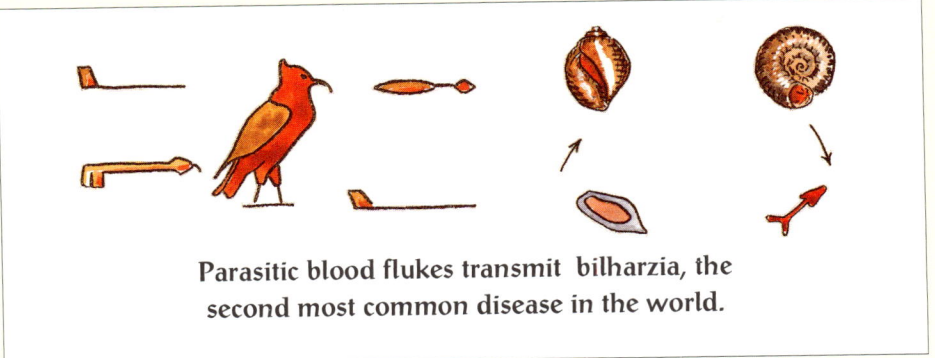

Parasitic blood flukes transmit bilharzia, the second most common disease in the world.

can lead to inflammation of the entire pelvic region. Kidney failure eventually results in death as poisonous body wastes accumulate in the blood.

Treatment

The drug niridazole is often recommended to substantially reduce blood fluke egg output, but there are often side effects such as mental confusion, psychosis, and, less commonly, convulsions. Treatment with the newly discovered drug praziquantel, which paralyzes the worms, making them vulnerable to the body's defense mechanisms, has proven highly successful. The drug is well tolerated and fast acting, but even successfully treated persons can experience relapses and easily become reinfected.

Prevention

- No drugs are presently available to prevent the infection. If you must wade in fresh water in these regions of the world, wear high, waterproof boots. Otherwise, stay away from riverbanks. If you accidentally come in contact with fresh water, dry off thoroughly and then immediately rub your skin with alcohol. Water for bathing and washing should be boiled or chlorinated. Avoid fresh fruits and uncooked vegetables in these parts of the world. Wear rubber gloves if you must put your hands in water.

BOOMSLANG

HOW IT GETS PEOPLE

Dispholidus typus

CLIMATIC ZONE

HABITAT

HABITAT

RATING

The boomslang is said to be rather shy and docile, and yet it is rightly considered to be an extremely dangerous snake. When threatened, its neck will inflate, and it will open its jaws so wide that the fangs in the rear of the upper jaw point straight out, allowing the boomslang to literally thrust forward and stab its victim. After striking its prey, the boomslang clamps its gaping mouth shut and chews the victim's flesh, injecting a large dose of lethal venom through the fangs at the back of the mouth. Envenomization is not as efficient as it is with the strike of a snake with fangs in the front of its mouth, but the boomslang's venom is just as deadly. One boomslang inflicted a fatal bite after embedding only one fang, and that for not much more than one second.

Boomslang

One unusual characteristic of boomslang envenomization is that the initial symptoms are followed by a period of remission. The unfortunate victim feels much better for a time, unaware of what awaits him. A 16-year-old South African boy was bitten on the hand while collecting birds' eggs from a nest. He was treated and felt well enough to go out the next day. Worried, his parents went to look for him, only to find him lying unconscious on the ground. He was carried inside and died shortly thereafter.

Another boomslang victim was the famed American herpetologist Karl Patterson Schmidt, curator of the Chicago Field Museum, who died 24 hours after being bitten. Only two hours before his death he felt well enough to call the museum to say that he would be at work the next day.

Even stranger than this period of remission is the fact that some boomslangs are born with two heads, each one acting as an independent being. One head might try to bite into its prey while the other head tries to stop it and take the victim for itself, apparently unaware that either way the prey will end up in the same stomach. In nature these terrifying

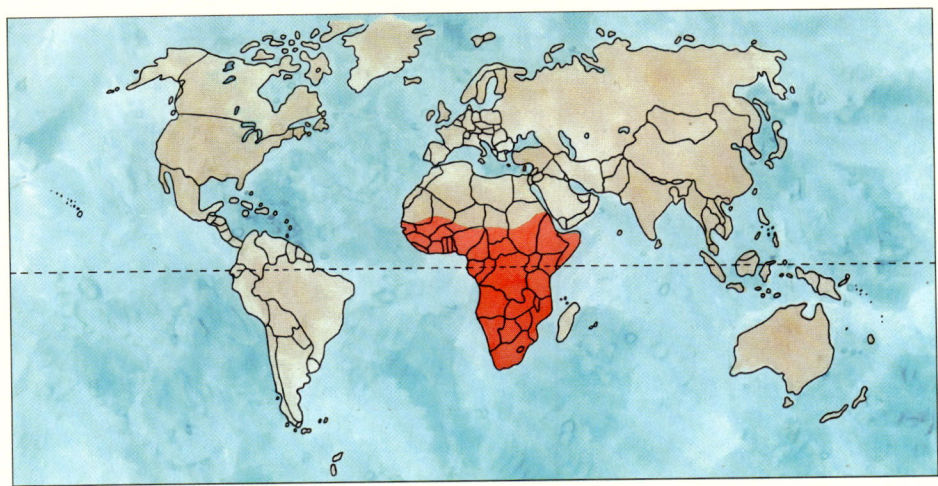

Dangerous Reptilian Creatures

mutants do not live very long, yet they have haunted people's imaginations for centuries and entered the mythology of many cultures.

Name/Description

The boomslang, or *Dispholidus typus*, is a member of the Colubridae family of snakes. It is a diurnal creature, meaning that it is active in the daytime. It is also arboreal. Considered to be rather docile, it has nevertheless proven to be fatal to many humans. An opisthoglyph, or rear-fanged snake, it has grooved teeth, and its fangs are small, short, and fragile. Usually about three and one-quarter feet long, boomslangs have been measured at over six and a half feet. Varying in color from brown to bright green, it has narrow scales. It feeds mostly on birds and their eggs, but also on frogs and chameleons.

Toxicology

The chemistry of the boomslang venom is not well understood. At first the victim's blood has a tendency to clot, but the venom also seems to have anticoagulant properties that reverse this initial clotting process.

Symptoms

At the site of the bite there will be pain, with some swelling and discoloration. About an hour later the victim will suffer from dizziness, severe headache, nausea, vomiting, and acute abdominal pain. At this stage the symptoms may disappear for several hours. As the venom spreads, the original clotting reverses itself, and there is profuse bleeding, at first from any open cuts and then from all body openings. This leads to a severe drop in blood pressure, and eventually death.

Prevention and Treatment

See Snakebites, page 116.

Boomslang

Immediately before death, boomslang bite victims ooze blood from every orifice of their body.

One characteristic of boomslang poisoning is the illusion of complete recovery, followed by sudden relapse and death.

BUSHMASTER

HOW IT GETS PEOPLE

Lachesis mutus

HOW IT GETS PEOPLE

HABITAT

HABITAT

HABITAT

CLIMATIC ZONE

RATING

Known as "the lonely, deadly danger of the remote jungle," the bushmaster is a powerful, formidable, deadly pit viper. It is in fact the largest of all pit vipers and the largest venomous snake in the Western Hemisphere. Its genus name, *Lachesis*, is that of one of the three Fates of Greek mythology, the one who determined the length of the thread of life. If a bushmaster bites you, that thread could be very short. You could be dead within a half hour. Although bushmasters range widely through the remote, mountainous jungles of tropical Central and South America, they are not very common. Active mainly at night and rare, their

Bushmaster

encounters with human beings are very infrequent. But these bold and dangerous pit vipers will stalk an intruder in their territory. Like other pit vipers, the bushmaster uses the heat-sensitive pits on either side of its head to locate prey. With proportions close to that of a rattlesnake, its tail ends in a horny spine that, although it cannot be rattled, does make a loud warning sound when shaken. In Brazil, where it is the subject of much folklore, the bushmaster is also known as the *surucucu*. The surucucu is said to be able to extinguish fire and to suckle from a cow or a sleeping woman, supposedly closing her infant's mouth so it will not cry and awaken her as it takes the milk.

Although its evil reputation is somewhat exaggerated, the bushmaster is quite deadly. Able to strike rapidly, it has a reach of three to four feet—more than a third of its body length. With extremely long fangs and the ability to deliver a massive dose of venom, the bushmaster has caused many deaths and is certainly not something to be toyed with. Yet that is exactly what a very silly—and incredibly lucky—couple once did. An employee of the Villa Artega Rubber Station in Antioquia, Colombia, was bathing in a stream with his wife when he saw a snake.

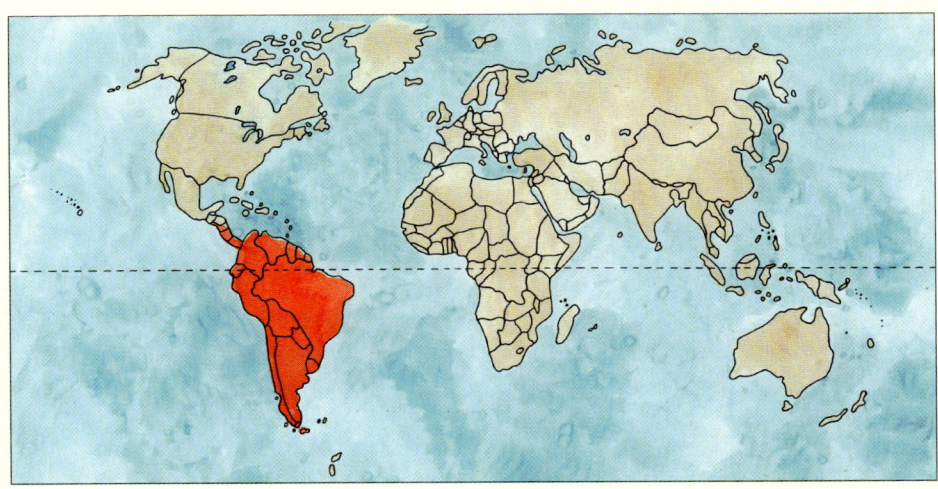

Dangerous Reptilian Creatures

Mistaking it for a nontoxic boa, he decided that it would make a nice addition to the collection of herpetologist Raymond Stadelman. Fashioning a noose from a shoelace, the couple dragged the reluctant beast along a dusty road. They encountered an Indian who told them that their boa was actually the dreaded bushmaster. The wife left the scene. The husband picked up the snake with the help of another workman and carried it to the site of the Stadelman collection, nearly strangling the reptile in the process. That neither husband nor wife was bitten after manhandling the snake so crudely is quite miraculous.

Name/Description

The bushmaster (*Lachesis mutus*) is a large, poisonous snake of the family Crotalidae and is related to the rattlesnake. The only species of its genus, it has enormous venom glands and very long fangs. A pit viper, the bushmaster has a bold pattern of dark, diamond-shaped, reddish brown blotches on a gray or brown background. It is the only egg-laying pit viper in the New World. It is mostly active at night and will not appear in bright daylight. The bushmaster is usually eight to nine feet long and feeds mainly on rodents. It is often found in the abandoned burrows of small mammals.

Toxicology

Bushmaster venom attacks both body tissues and the blood. The principal toxic compound is protease. Fatalities usually occur within a few hours.

Symptoms

Bushmaster envenomization is similar to that of other vipers. First there is pain around the bite. The area around the wound may then become temporarily numb. There is swelling and discoloration of the skin. How rapidly these symptoms appear depends on the severity of the bite. The victim may also experience weakness, fainting, sweating, thirst, nausea,

Bushmaster

The deadly bushmaster has extremely long
fangs that carry massive doses of venom.

vomiting, and loss of consciousness. Consciousness is usually regained after a few minutes, but there follows a period of falling blood pressure, elevated temperature, and sometimes violent spasms and convulsions. Even with mild envenomization, there will be some bleeding and death of tissue around the bite.

Treatment

An antivenin for bushmaster poisoning is available. See Snakebites, page 116.

COBRA

HOW IT GETS PEOPLE

Genus Naja

HOW IT GETS PEOPLE

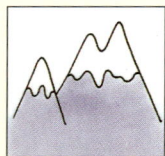
HABITAT

HABITAT

HABITAT

HABITAT

HABITAT

CLIMATIC ZONE

CLIMATIC ZONE

RATING

It may seem romantic to wander, as did E. M. Forster's fictional Mrs. Ashcroft, amid the ancient ruins of India, but you should be warned that in doing so you may make a swift departure to your next incarnation. Crumbling monuments are one of the favorite haunts of the nervous, excitable, and deadly cobra. Nocturnal—that is, active at night—the

Cobra

cobra also likes to lurk in the roofs and dark corners of native huts, waiting for rodents. It is equally fond of frogs, lizards, and insects, and it will even climb trees in pursuit of birds' eggs. Cobras like to drink water, although, like most reptiles, they can go for many months without food or drink.

The Indians have a reverence for the cobra, which they regard as a powerful and dangerous divinity to be fed and protected. Each February at the Nagapančami Festival, offerings of milk and plantains are made to the serpents. The Subramaniah Temple in Mysore was erected to the glory of the cobra and is tended by Brahmin priests. The Indian government has tried to fight this superstition and to exterminate cobras by offering a substantial reward for each head turned in. But deaths from cobra bites are still common. Most frequently, bare-legged farmers are bitten at night when they go out to deposit their "night soil" on their fields.

Indian snake charmers, no matter how clever, cannot make cobras dance to their music. What actually happens is that the snake, which has usually been defanged, is hypnotized by the moving tip of the snake

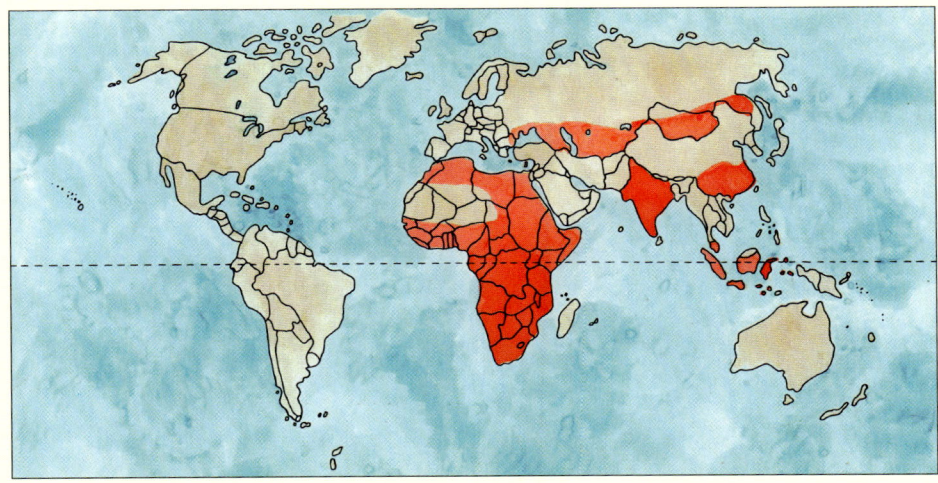

Dangerous Reptilian Creatures

charmer's flute. Snake keepers in China have learned to grab a swaying, upright cobra at the throat by rhythmically moving their other hand in the air at a safe distance. This requires a great deal of skill, because a cobra can strike a blow from more than three feet away. Even the most skillful handler does not always get away with it. China reports approximately 30,000 deaths from snakebite each year.

A cobra may spit venom at its victim rather than bite, and this is said to cause an intense, burning pain in the eyes. Envenomization from a bite, however, produces a different effect, with the venom acting as a kind of anesthetic. Carl F. Kauffeld, former director of the Staten Island Zoo, has written of his own cobra envenomization, "I was sinking into a state that could not be called unconsciousness, but one in which I was no longer aware of what was going on about me. . . . I felt no anxiety; I felt no pain. . . . I only felt a complete and utter lassitude in which nothing seemed to matter—not at all unpleasant if this is the way death comes from cobra poisoning."

The cobra's strike is preceeded by a fearful hiss, the same noise we make when we want to hush a room—*shhh*! (Our instinctive fear of this noise, according to the popular science writer Carl Sagan, can be traced back to the time when all-powerful reptiles dominated the world. Our small mammalian ancestors were terrorized by the slightest hiss from these repulsive creatures, their worst enemies.)

Name/Description

The name of this snake comes from the Portuguese word *cobra*, meaning "serpent." The name of the genus, *Naja*, is from the Sanskrit word *naga*, meaning "snake." The various species of Asiatic and African cobras are members of the Elapidae family, snakes whose interior ribs can be raised and brought forward, expanding and flattening the neck into a broad disk or hood. Markings on the back of the neck are so geographically

Cobra

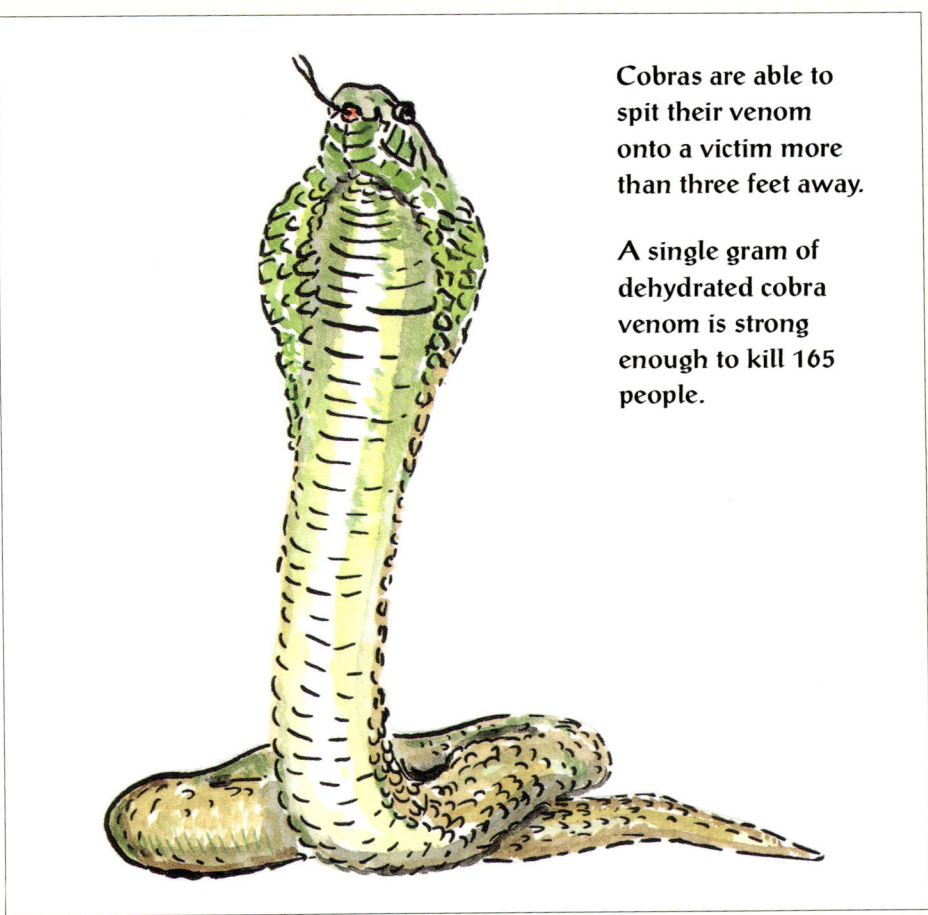

Cobras are able to spit their venom onto a victim more than three feet away.

A single gram of dehydrated cobra venom is strong enough to kill 165 people.

specific that they can be used to identify a species. Usually measuring between 4 and 8 feet, king cobras can grow up to 18 feet. The cobra's fangs are located in the upper jaw, and the poison gland is about the size of an almond. The female lays her eggs in holes in dead trees, in old buildings, or under dead brush. The cobra feeds mainly on rodents, small reptiles, and insects.

Dangerous Reptilian Creatures

Toxicology

Before venom will flow from the poison gland and enter the victim's wound, the cobra's fangs must be solidly implanted in flesh and its jaws firmly pressed together, so a glancing strike is not likely to be deadly. Nevertheless, the bite of a vigorous cobra can prove fatal in just a few minutes. There are three species of cobra that can spit their venom. Strong muscles around the poison gland contract and force the ejection of a fine spray of venom as much as five to seven feet away. Spitting cobras tend to aim at reflective surfaces, such as the human eye, and they are very accurate.

Symptoms

Symptoms vary with the species but generally include pain radiating from the site of the bite, swelling, edema—the abnormal accumulation of fluid in the body's cells—and progressive numbness around the wound. Nausea and sleepiness follow. There is also progressive paralysis of the facial muscles, tongue, and larynx. The eyes appear glazed and cease their movements, and the eyelids begin to droop. The victim remains conscious but can speak only with great difficulty. Blood pressure drops, the limbs become paralyzed, the chest muscles stop functioning, and the victim ultimately dies of asphyxiation. This last, agonizing stage is accompanied by violent vomiting. See also Snakebites, page 116.

Treatment

Antivenin is widely available. Force the wound to bleed. Do not give the victim alcohol. Try to get the victim to drink a beverage with a high

Cobra

caffeine content, such as black coffee. If the victim was only sprayed in the eyes, wash the venom out with ordinary milk or administer a weak solution of permanganate (0.001%, or 1 part permanganate to 1,000 parts of water). See also Snakebites, page 116.

Prevention
- Try to stay above or behind a cobra, as it can only strike in a forward and downward direction.

COPPERHEAD

HOW IT GETS PEOPLE

Agkistrodon contortrix

CLIMATIC ZONE

HABITAT

HABITAT

HABITAT

HABITAT

HABITAT

HABITAT

RATING

If you decide to cruise the rivers and wetlands of the southeastern United States, be careful. You are probably in copperhead territory. The banks of these regions echo with the sounds of frantic weekend adventurers trying desperately to club a surprised copperhead to death with oars and paddles. But few are successful, and many fall victim to the snake that undoubtedly bites more people in the United States than any other snake. The southern, the northern, the broad-backed, and the

Copperhead

osage copperhead are the four subspecies of copperheads found in the southern and eastern areas of the United States. Commonly called the chunkhead because of its large head, the copperhead's other common names—red oak snake, poplar leaf snake, and white oak snake—reflect its magnificent adaptive coloration. Copperheads are strikingly beautiful snakes, with narrow or broad reddish brown or cinnamon bands arranged in an irregular zigzag pattern over a gray or pinkish background. The upper lip and lower jaw are lighter in color than the coppery top of the head. The copperhead spends much of its time slithering across the foliage-covered forest floor, and its unique coloration helps to camouflage it. It can remain motionless, coiled and waiting for prey, making it a very real danger to unsuspecting hikers.

Though the copperhead lacks a proper rattle, it does vibrate its tail when angry or excited. This action may produce a clear buzzing sound if the snake is coiled on dry leaves or grass. Copperheads are said to have a beautiful mating ritual in which the male and female move as one. The female leads and the male follows, exhibiting a "fluency that has to be seen to be appreciated."

Dangerous Reptilian Creatures

Copperheads are extremely adaptable and are not found just in the country. They often live in well-populated urban areas and seem to have a habit of moving into territories where rattlesnakes have been driven away.

Name/Description

Copperheads comprise four subspecies of *Agkistrodon contortrix* and are found mainly in the eastern half of the United States. Moderate in size, the adults range from 22 to 53 inches in length, with the males larger than the females. The body is comparatively stout, and the head is broad and triangular. Handsomely colored, the snakes have a copperlike tinge and large brownish crossbands on a paler background. The underside is rose colored with two rows of dark spots, like the cottonmouth. The under part of the tail has a single row of plates for two-thirds of its length; the remaining third has two rows. Food consists mainly of small rodents, but copperheads will also eat large insects and caterpillars. Females bear 8 to 12 live young, which can be identified by the sulfur yellow color of the tips of their tails. Copperheads are active at night in warm weather and active during the day in cool weather.

Toxicology

The venom of the copperhead is not particularly toxic, and it is rare that a copperhead bite leads to death, though it can be quite painful.

Symptoms

Symptoms vary depending on the amount of venom injected, but generally copperhead bites cause immediate swelling, pain, and edema. The symptoms manifest themselves within 15 minutes. Untreated, the swelling progresses rapidly and within hours may involve the entire

Copperhead

Copperheads attack more people annually in the United States than any other snake.

limb. The lymph nodes may become enlarged and tender. A rise in body temperature, weakness, a rapid and weak pulse, fainting, sweating, nausea, and vomiting may occur. The victim may experience shock and have difficulty breathing, but will usually recover.

Treatment and Prevention
See Snakebites, page 116.

CORAL SNAKE

Genera Micrurus, Micruroides, and Leptomicrurus

  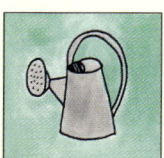  
HOW IT GETS PEOPLE — HABITAT — HABITAT — HABITAT — HABITAT

HABITAT — CLIMATIC ZONE — CLIMATIC ZONE — RATING

In many parts of the southeastern United States, children sing a little ditty about a type of candy cane that is far from sweet: "Red and black, friend of Jack. Red and yellow, kill a fellow." These children are learning the different color combinations that distinguish the eastern coral snake, considered by some to be the most dangerous snake in the United States, from its nonpoisonous mimics, the scarlet snake and the milk snake. Other children are told that when they see a snake colored like a candy cane they should think of traffic lights—red for stop and yellow for caution. If these two bands of colors are touching on a snake, watch out!

    The coral snake's small mouth and short fangs make it difficult for the snake to bite most larger parts of the human anatomy, but it seems quite adept at biting, holding on to, and chewing toes and fingers. Chewing helps the coral snake work its venom into the tissue around a

Coral Snake

bite. The coral snake holds on so tightly that the victim has to violently shake his or her arm before it will let go of a finger or thumb. Often the snake has to be pulled off, a sensation that has been described by a victim as "separating Velcro."

Most bites occur in the spring and fall, and in the majority of cases, it is the victim who goes after the snake, either mistaking it for a nonvenomous mimic or displaying a reckless, drunken bravado. Amazingly, in one study of eastern coral snakebites, more than one-third of the victims were intoxicated. In one case, a drunken farmhand attempted to win a wager by handling a coral snake. He was bitten, and the snake was pulled off. Though his symptoms developed slowly, he was paralyzed for six days and could only move the muscles of his diaphragm and hands. He eventually recovered but did not regain normal muscle strength for a month.

In another case, a suburban teenager picked up a coral snake and was bitten. She immediately went to a clinic but was not treated because she showed no symptoms. Thirteen hours after the bite, she suddenly became totally paralyzed and was unable to breathe. She was treated, but except for the ability to rotate her left foot, she remained unable to

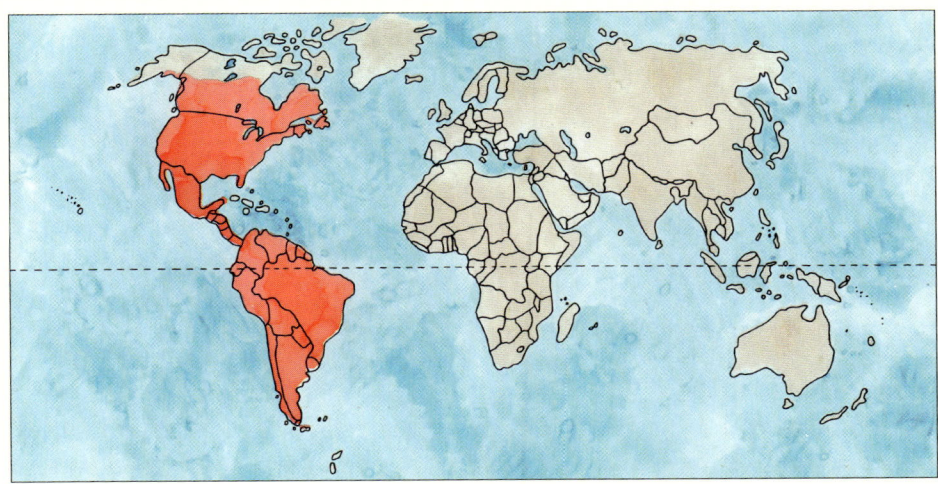

Dangerous Reptilian Creatures

move for the next five days. The girl did not fully recover for another six weeks.

Name/Description

There are about 50 species of coral snakes grouped into three genera: *Micrurus*, *Micruroides*, and *Leptomicrurus*, and all of them are extremely poisonous. They prefer tropical or subtropical climates and are found throughout the warmer regions of North and South America. They are brilliantly banded with alternating red, black, and yellowish white rings. Two to four feet in length, they have black snouts with two short fangs attached to the front of the upper jaw. Though the fangs are their only teeth, they chew when they bite. They like to burrow into damp spots under logs, rocks, and trash piles. Coral snakes prowl by day, especially in the morning. The females are oviparous, that is, they produce eggs that hatch after leaving the mother's body, rather than giving birth to live young. Coral snakes feed chiefly on lizards, frogs, other small snakes, insects, and occasionally on young birds. When threatened or restrained, the coral snake may thrust its tail upward over its body, with the tip curved into a sort of ball that can be mistaken for the head, to confuse its attacker.

Toxicology

The coral snake's venom is neurotoxic, meaning that it affects the nervous system. The principle toxic compounds are cholinesterase, hyaluronidase, L-amino-acid oxidase, and other enzymes. There is envenomization in 75 percent of *Micrurus* bites. A large coral snake can easily inject four and a half times the lethal dose for humans. The venom of some species works incredibly fast; its most toxic ingredients are absorbed directly into the bloodstream and quickly disseminated throughout the body.

Symptoms

Depending on the species, the onset of symptoms can be instantaneous and the victim can die within minutes, or symptoms may not appear for

Coral Snake

Coral snakes are quite adept at clinging to and chewing on human fingers and toes.

as long as 12 hours. Generally there is numbness without pain at the site of the bite. Victims will experience headache, swelling of the face and lips, increased prickliness of the skin, sore throat, drooping eyelids, abnormal sensitivity to light, vomiting, rapid heart rate, backache, irritability, and uncontrollable salivation. The immediate cause of death is usually respiratory paralysis. Even mild envenomization can result in a major disruption of the nervous system, including paralysis of the cranial nerves. But with minor envenomization there are no permanent effects, and the symptoms disappear after several months.

Treatment
If there is major envenomization, especially from the bite of an eastern coral snake, ordinary first aid is largely ineffective because the toxins are so fast acting. Do not give the victim anything to eat or drink and get him to a hospital quickly. Since 1967, an antivenin for *M. fulvius fulvius* has been available in the United States, though treatment with antivenin does not rapidly reverse symptoms. See also Snakebites, page 116.

Prevention
- Remember the little jingle, and avoid any snake with alternating red and yellow rings.
- Do not go near any brilliantly ringed snake, even if you *know* it is a mimic, as did so many other—now deceased—snake experts.

COTTONMOUTH

HOW IT GETS PEOPLE

Agkistrodon piscivorous

CLIMATIC ZONE

HABITAT

HABITAT

RATING

The cottonmouth is extremely dangerous. An aggressive snake, it usually lives near the water where hiding places are abundant. Because it gives no warning before striking, it is also known as the "rattlesnake without rattles." Very large and heavy-bodied, it carries a large load of venom.

Byron Dalrymple, a writer for *Field and Stream* magazine who has had more encounters with cottonmouths than he would like to remember, was fishing for bass one day when his line got caught in some hyacinths. As he knelt over the prow of his boat to free the lure, a huge cottonmouth suddenly reared up and opened its mouth, showing Dalrymple the cottonlike lining of its throat—the origin of its name. Luckily, this cottonmouth backed down, and Dalrymple paddled away. His next encounter with the snake was in Florida when he went out one night to photograph a hooting owl. Just outside his door, he ran the beam of his flashlight across the deck. It was literally crawling with cottonmouths. On another occasion, when he was fishing in a Georgia river, Dalrymple

Cottonmouth

saw a guide with a middle-aged couple in an old flat-bottomed boat. The woman suddenly stood up and reached out for a tree limb to steady herself. The guide shrieked, "Sit down!" and swerved the boat so fast he almost dumped her into the river. On the branch she had tried to grab was a cottonmouth that Dalrymple described as being "as thick as my wrist."

Cottonmouths love fresh water and are often found in and about canals, rice fields, drainage ditches, flooded fields, and wetlands. They are good swimmers. They have also been known to crawl into moving boats. But sometimes they are deliberately and maliciously put into unnatural hiding places. During the summers of 1964 and 1965, civil rights workers in Mississippi found that cottonmouths and other reptiles had been placed in their automobiles. Fortunately, no one was bitten, and it was even said that some FBI agents, "in a particularly macho gesture," killed the snakes, then cooked and ate them.

Death from cottonmouth envenomization sounds like a nightmare, but it is not always the venom that kills you. A 21-year-old man was bitten on the lower left leg while swimming. Within two hours he was

Dangerous Reptilian Creatures

treated by a doctor who saw redness and swelling around the fang marks and based his treatment on the young man's complaints of "severe pain, weakness, and a feeling of excessive thirst." Even after treatment involving suction, plasma transfusions, and antivenin, the young man remained in serious condition. Soon his whole leg and lower trunk was swollen, the tendons of the affected leg were exposed, and there was extensive gangrene. One week later the patient began to complain of new symptoms—headache, a stiff neck, and a feeling of restlessness, followed by difficulty in swallowing and convulsions. He died of tetanus within 24 hours.

Name/Description
The cottonmouth (*Agkistrodon piscivorous*) grows to between three and six feet in length. It is a dark olive–green, banded pit viper. Semiaquatic, it has a very heavy body, a broad, flat head, and a distinct neck. It has a characteristic stripe extending from the eye to the corner of the mouth. When disturbed, a cottonmouth will stand its ground and open its mouth wide, displaying its white lining. These pit vipers swim with their heads out of water, aided in breathing by a slightly upturned snout, but under most circumstances they cannot strike while in the water. Often they will lie on overhead branches or at the water's edge, waiting for birds or small animals to come to drink. The venom of the young cottonmouth is more potent than that of the adult.

Toxicology
The principle toxic compounds of cottonmouth venom are cephalinase, cholinesterase, hyaluronidase, and lacithinase. The venom causes severe tissue damage and scarring.

Symptoms
Symptoms usually begin to develop within 10 minutes of being bitten. There is immediate local pain, extensive swelling, the appearance of

Cottonmouth

Young cottonmouth snakes possess more toxic venom than do fully grown ones.

black-and-blue marks, gangrene, nausea, and vomiting. In severe cases there will be internal bleeding before death.

Treatment
See Snakebites, page 116.

Prevention
- Know the cottonmouth's habits. Fishermen should be careful when retrieving lures hung on branches, bushes, or floating vegetation. In cottonmouth country, bang a long pole against the trees ahead of you as you walk. Never reach for anything in the bushes at or above ground level without carefully looking first.

CROCODILES AND ALLIGATORS

HOW IT GETS PEOPLE

Crocodylidae and Alligatoridae

CLIMATIC ZONE

HABITAT

HABITAT

HABITAT

RATING

The fear of being eaten by an animal seems much greater than the fear of just being killed by one, especially if one is about to be eaten by one of these angry-looking reptiles. The 18th-century naturalist William Bartram was accused of having "sullied their name with over-heated prose," but most witnesses to crocodile and alligator attacks would probably agree with his description of one: "The horrid noise of their closing jaws, the floods of water and blood rushing out of their mouths, and the clouds of vapor issuing from their wide nostrils were truly frightful." They are indiscriminate eaters, we are told, whose taste in food, says "Mr. Ned"—Edward A. McIlhenny of the famed Bayou-country Tabasco sauce family—includes "everything living in range of its jaws that flies, walks, swims, or crawls."

A sampling of their eclectic taste was found in the stomach of an old saltwater crocodile that had been killed after devouring an Australian aborigine. It contained, as well as the victim's remains, a four-gallon

Crocodiles and Alligators

drum containing two blankets. These reptiles think nothing of taking on a large mammal such as a horse or water buffalo. In the words of one witness to such an attack, "with murderous jaws the huge reptile seizes the buffalo by the nose. Using its powerful tail to throw itself into a violent roll, the crocodile twists the buffalo and . . . drags it deeper and deeper into the water."

But much too often the victim is another type of mammal. On the Nile River alone, crocodiles probably kill about 1,000 people a year. One 15-foot crocodile, shot on the Kihange River in central Africa, was supposed to have killed 400 people. People have been snatched out of canoes when foolishly trailing their hands in the water. A game warden in Uganda, C. R. S. Pitman, described such a scene: "The tragedy is instantaneous. One moment all is peaceful, then without warning the hand is seized, the horrid head jerks sideways with astonishing violence, and the victim is not dragged but literally hauled out of the boat, it's the work of a second." And once they have you, they do not like to let go.

The largest such reptile is the estuarine or saltwater crocodile *Crocodylus porosus* of Oceania, the island chains of the South Pacific. Adult males average 14 to 16 feet in length and weigh between 700 and 1,100

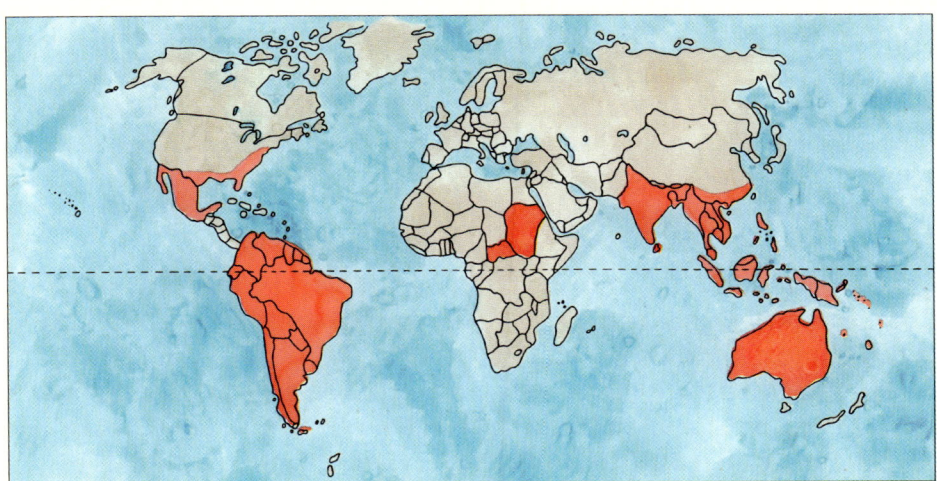

Dangerous Reptilian Creatures

pounds. A specimen more than 28 feet in length and weighing 4,400 pounds was found and photographed in Norman River, Australia, in 1957. It is hard to imagine why anyone would want one of these killers as a pet, but President John Quincy Adams kept his pet alligator in the East Room of the White House.

Name/Description

Crocodile comes from the Greek word *krokodilos*, meaning "lizard." Alligator comes from the Spanish word *el lagarto*, also meaning "lizard." Crocodiles and alligators are large, long-bodied, amphibious reptiles of tropical and subtropical waters. Long, narrow, triangular-shaped heads feature massive jaws with cone-shaped teeth. The closing force of these jaws has been measured at 1,200 pounds per square inch, but the jaws once closed, a man of ordinary strength can keep them shut with the grip of one hand. Alligators and crocodiles are egg layers and are territorial, especially during breeding season. Lethargic during the day and active mainly at night, they like to float along and drift with the currents, but when excited they can move surprisingly fast both in the water and on land. They have a thick, horny skin composed of scales and plates, and their long, powerful tail is serrated. Sensory receptors are located in the sides of the jaws. When they submerge, an array of valves and flaps in the nose, throat, and ears snap closed, and transparent membranes close over their eyes. Crocodiles and alligators are the largest living reptiles in the world today. They can live to be 50 years old.

    Crocodiles are somewhat larger and more aggressive than alligators and are savage fighters when agitated or captured. Tannish gray or dark green, they have long, tapering snouts and large teeth in the lower jaws that protrude prominently when their mouths are closed. Their voice is a low rumble or growl.

    Alligators differ from crocodiles in that they have shorter and blunter snouts, with no conspicuous teeth in the lower jaw. Usually black, they prefer fresh water. Their bellowing roar can be heard for a mile.

Crocodiles and Alligators

Crocodiles and alligators can digest an entire horse or water buffalo in just two days.

Injury

Crocodiles and alligators usually attack from the side or from below, holding on to their victims with their powerful jaws and dragging them underwater to drown them. To drag their victims under, they fold their legs against their bodies and rapidly rotate underwater by movements of their powerful tails. Able to stay underwater longer than most land animals, they usually wait until their prey is dead before dismembering it. If there are any remains, they may be taken back to a den on a nearby bank and saved for a later meal. Many attacks by such reptiles are not fatal, but produce severe lacerations, punctures, compound fractures, and secondary infections.

Treatment

See Bites, Gorings, Maulings, and Shock, page 121.

DIAMONDBACK RATTLESNAKE

Crotalus adamanteus and Crotalus atrox

HOW IT GETS PEOPLE

HABITAT

CLIMATIC ZONE

RATING

Rattlesnakes have played an extraordinary role in the history and mythology of North America. Native Americans worshiped the rattlesnake and believed that it possessed supernatural powers like those attributed to cobras in India. Rattlesnakes were featured on the flags of many of the early colonies. There were even rattlesnake cults. One such cult appeared in the southeastern United States around the turn of the 20th century. At least 20 members died from fatal bites suffered during the cult's rituals, among them George Went Hensley, the cult's founder.

Herpetologist Roger A. Caras states that rattlesnakes have "clearly the most advanced and efficient biting mechanism," with long fangs at the front of the mouth that can be folded up into the roof of the mouth when not needed. With a system similar to a cartridge clip in a semi-automatic pistol, rattlers may have as many as six additional fangs on either side of their jaws, which can be brought into play when one of the two primary fangs is damaged.

Diamondback rattlesnakes are considered to be the most dangerous snakes in the United States, with the eastern diamondback ranking

Diamondback Rattlesnake

"among the world's deadliest snakes," according to Caras. Its cousin, the western diamondback, is known as a very aggressive snake, having a hair-trigger readiness to strike. Nor is the western diamondback afraid of crawling out into the open, even around populated ranches.

"Rattlers" have been used in murder attempts, though they have sometimes bitten the would-be murderer instead of the chosen victim. Sometimes they have simply failed to live up to their dreaded reputation. One California man sought to kill his wife with a rattlesnake, but he found the reptile unequal to the task and eventually drowned the unfortunate woman. In 1978 two other Californians attempted to murder an attorney by placing a large rattlesnake in his mailbox. He was severely bitten but recovered. The men were arrested and charged with attempted murder.

Practical jokes involving snakes have long been commonplace around army barracks and country schools, and here again it is not always the intended victim who gets hurt. A Texas cowhand is said to have killed a cowboy who had placed a small rattlesnake, with its mouth sewed up, inside the cowhand's boot. At a New Year's Eve party in Los Angeles, the host decided to exhibit his pet rattlesnake to his guests. As

Dangerous Reptilian Creatures

he took the snake from its cage, it bit him on the thumb. Absentmindedly, he handed the snake to a guest, who thought he was being offered a can of beer. This man was also bitten and dropped the snake in the lap of a third person, who was bitten in a matter of seconds. The snake's owner sought no medical attention and apparently had not been envenomated. The second and third men, however, received moderate doses of venom and recovered only after hospitalization and treatment with antivenin.

A rattler does not have to be alive to bite you. James A. Oliver, former director of the American Museum of Natural History, has confirmed cases of rattlers inflicting bites through spasmodic movements of the jaws after they were dead.

Name/Description

Rattlesnakes are thick-bodied, venomous snakes with large heads, distinct necks, and horny, interlocking joints at the ends of their tails that make sharp, rattling sounds when shaken. Diamondbacks vary from other rattlers because of distinctive diamond- or lozenge-shaped markings on their backs, and they usually have two white stripes running from the eyes to the corner of the mouth. In the southeastern United States, the eastern diamondback rattlesnake (*Crotalus adamanteus*) grows up to eight feet in length. It is also known as the Florida diamondback rattlesnake. Its cousin, the western diamondback rattlesnake (*Crotalus atrox*), although smaller in length and possessing shorter fangs and smaller poison glands, is the cause of more serious snakebites than all other species of rattlers. Also known as the coontail rattler for the alternating black and white rings encircling its tail, its venom is more potent, and it is much more temperamental and easily excited than the eastern diamondback.

Toxicology

Rattlesnake venom poisons the blood and destroys tissue. The eastern diamondback's venom contains cephalinase, cholinesterase, and hyaluronidase. The western diamondback's venom contains bradykinogen,

Diamondback Rattlesnake

Rattlesnakes are considered the most dangerous snakes in the United States.

cholinesterase, hyaluronidase, L-amino-acid oxidase, and other substances.

Symptoms
Symptoms of rattlesnake envenomization include local pain, edema or swelling, internal bleeding, dryness of the mouth, vomiting, shock, anemia, tingling sensations, blood in the feces, slurred speech, and finally loss of consciousness and death.

Treatment
An antivenin is available for all pit vipers. See Snakebites, page 116.

Prevention
- Never step or place a hand near or under a rock or a log in "rattler" country; go around.
- Be careful in and around abandoned buildings, which are havens for rodents, a favorite prey of rattlers.
- In hot, sunny weather, avoid the shadows.
- Do not forget that a rattler sounds much farther away than it really is.

FER-DE-LANCE

HOW IT GETS PEOPLE

Bothrops asper

CLIMATIC ZONE

HABITAT

HABITAT

HABITAT

RATING

In the 19th century, this particularly aggressive pit viper was the major cause of death for West Indian plantation workers. It was given the name *fer-de-lance,* the French for "spearhead," on the island of Martinique, where it was discovered by French Creoles, who also called it "the evil spirit of sugar plantations." So numerous were its victims that, in 1850, desperate plantation owners imported the mongoose, the natural enemy of the cobra, in the hope that it would eradicate this menace. But the two parties involved proved mutually disinterested, and the deaths of barefoot plantation workers continued.

With very large venom glands, long fangs, and an aggressive disposition, the fer–de–lance is a formidable adversary. It is one of the few snakes whose venom is both neurotoxic and hemotoxic, affecting the nervous system and destroying red blood cells. A prolific breeder, the

Fer-de-lance

female fer-de-lance gives birth to a litter of 60 to 70 newborns, each about a foot long, which are capable of dangerous bites. As with many pit vipers, the venom of the young snake is more potent than that of the adult.

If a fer-de-lance strikes a large blood vessel, the victim can die within 20 minutes. Active at night, the fer-de-lance waits in its lair until dusk and then noiselessly glides about in search of prey, feeling the ground with its forked tongue. When it encounters its prey, it will raise its head and coil itself, ready to strike with a venom of unbelievable potency.

The naturalist writer R. Ditmars recounts the story of yet another plantation worker who had been bitten by a fer-de-lance. He was brought home with a badly bleeding wound. The victim's wife washed the wound with water and called the local "snake doctor." In spite of his treatment, she was a widow two hours later. The next morning the wife also died, with the characteristic symptoms of fer-de-lance poisoning. Yet she had not been bitten. How was this possible? It appears that she had developed small abrasions on her fingers from handling coconuts, and the fatal venom must have entered her system when she was cleansing her husband's wound.

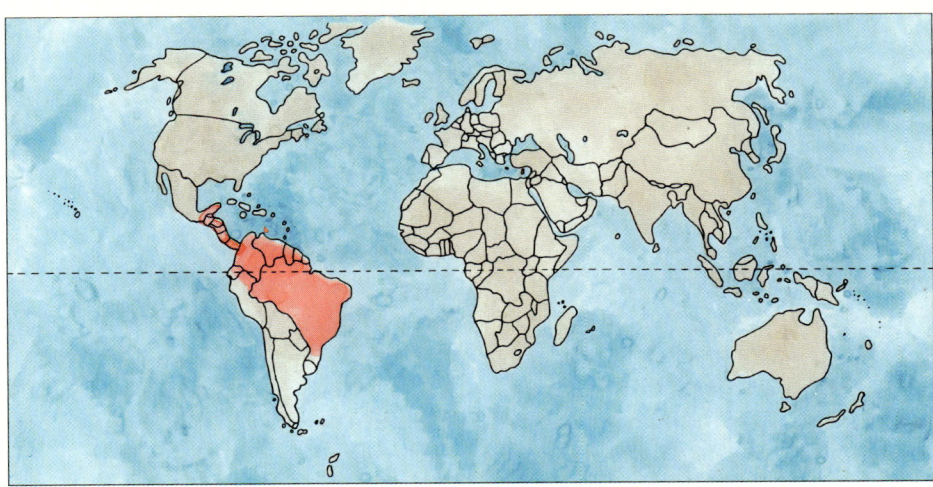

Dangerous Reptilian Creatures

The fer-de-lance is a large pit viper with a pointed, lance-shaped head. Deadly poisonous and not at all shy about striking, *Bothrops asper* usually feeds on rodents and small mammals. Like other pit vipers, it has hollow fangs and heat-sensing organs on either side of its head, which it uses to locate prey. Up to eight feet long and often as thick as a man's arm, it waits for prey, motionless, for long periods of time. Usually gray-olive brown or gray-green, the fer-de-lance has conspicuous dark, pale-edged, diamond-shaped blotches, though the precise patterns and colors are highly variable. In almost every country where it is found, the fer-de-lance has a different name, such as *barba amarilla* (yellow beard), for its yellowish throat and chin, and *terciopelo* (velvet snake). It is most prevalent around human settlements where trash and garbage attract small rodents, its favorite food.

Toxicology

The toxic compounds of fer-de-lance venom are cholinesterase, deoxyribonuclease, L-amino-acid oxidase, protease, and other enzymes that digest muscle tissue, destroy blood cells, and cause copious bleeding and edema. In addition, the venom often contains many species of infectious bacteria, including tetanus.

Symptoms

The initial bite may feel no more painful than the jab of a hypodermic needle. But soon there will be localized pain, intense bleeding, and severe swelling. An arm can swell to twice its normal size. The venom inhibits the clotting ability of the blood, and bleeding can occur from the internal organs, the gums, nose, mouth, eyes, ears, or rectum—anywhere but from the bite itself, which is usually too swollen to bleed freely. The hemorrhaging can progress into the muscular and nervous systems. Shock, respiratory distress, paralysis, and death may follow.

Fer-de-lance

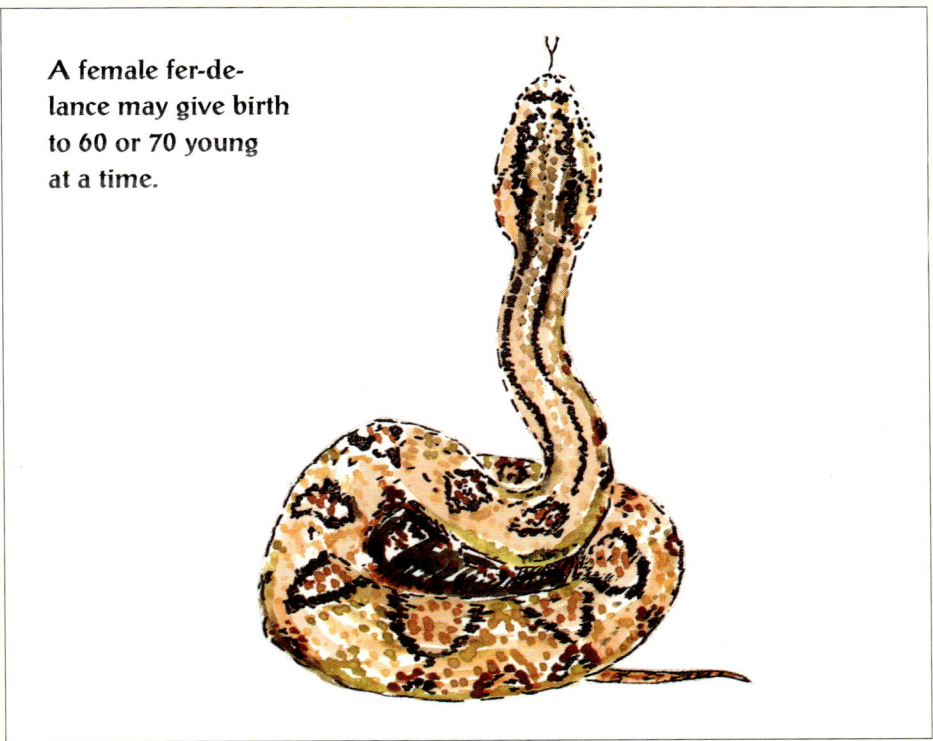

A female fer-de-lance may give birth to 60 or 70 young at a time.

Treatment
Under no circumstances should the "cut and suck" method be considered because of the danger of heavy bleeding. When pit viper antivenin or other drugs are administered intravenously, a new set of problems can occur because the needle has to be moved constantly to avoid the heavy bleeding it causes. Sometimes every vein in the arms, legs, and even in the feet must be used to administer sufficient antivenin.

Prevention
- For prevention, see Snakebites, page 116.

GABOON VIPER

HOW IT GETS PEOPLE

Bitis gabonica

CLIMATIC ZONE

HABITAT

HABITAT

HABITAT

RATING

The mighty Gaboon viper that roams the jungles of central Africa is probably the one snake that comes closest to delivering sudden death. Not only is it the largest of all vipers—only the bushmaster is comparable in size—it has the largest fangs of any snake in the world, up to two inches long. They can even pierce leather shoes. If a Gaboon viper bites someone on the foot or lower leg, it can almost bite through the limb, and if it bites the upper torso, its enormous fangs

Gaboon Viper

can inject venom deep into the victim's body, resulting in rapid and profound envenomization. The venom contains substances that affect both the nervous and circulatory systems, and even immediate treatment with antivenin becomes complicated. Gaboon viper bites have resulted in numerous tragic deaths, but many a person has been saved by a quick amputation of the affected finger, the most common place to be bitten.

Rather sluggish and without a pronounced tendency to bite, the Gaboon viper's placid temperament disguises its ability to make a lightning strike. When it does attack, it almost always hits its target. Most bites and fatalities occur when someone inadvertently steps on one of these well-camouflaged, sausagelike serpents lying almost invisible in the leaf litter on the forest floor. It possesses magnificent coloring, with patterns that have been compared to an oriental carpet. Known to dine on small antelope, Gaboon vipers have no trouble swallowing five-pound monkeys. The Gaboon viper is a puff adder, a snake that, when excited, will inflate itself to look more imposing. The Gaboon viper can inflate itself to twice its thickness.

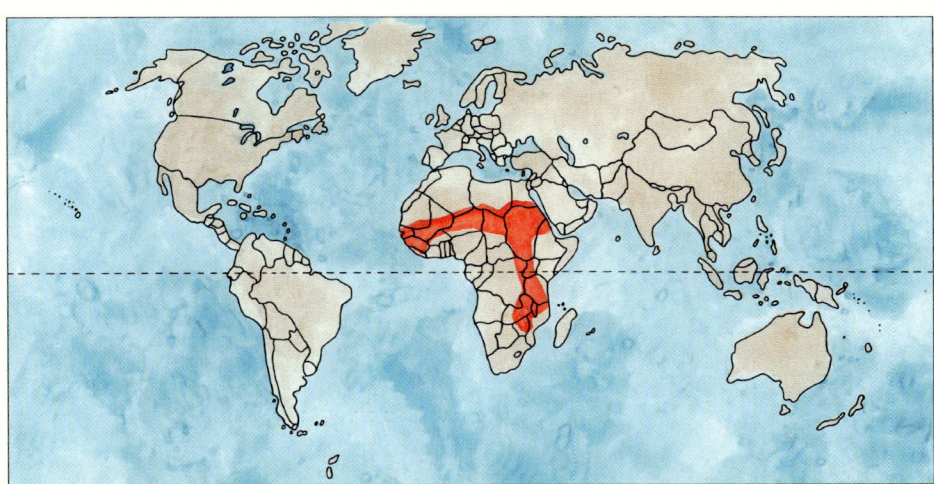

Dangerous Reptilian Creatures

Name/Description

The enormously heavy-bodied Gaboon viper (*Bitis gabonica*) is an extremely venomous tropical puff adder measuring up to six feet in length. Its triangular head, with vertical, elliptical eyes, sits atop a narrow neck. Gaboon viper populations can be quite large. In one area of Tanzania, herpetologist C. J. P. Ionides collected over 2,000 specimens, commenting that this did not appear to noticeably reduce the local population. The Gaboon viper is a sedentary creature, and at certain times of the year males are much more in evidence than females.

The Gaboon viper's coloration is a superb example of how a species adapts to its environment. Their markings make them virtually disappear in the shade of the jungle foliage. The entire body appears to be an intricate pattern of varying shades of brown, cream, and purple. Large vipers such as the Gaboon viper rarely move in the typical snakelike manner. Most snakes make S-curve movements as they slither across the ground, and a few move like inchworms, arching their bodies. Because Gaboon vipers are so heavy, they use their large belly scales to support the body via rib movements. They move in a straight line.

Toxicology

The Gaboon viper's venom both affects the nervous system and destroys red blood cells, which complicates the administering of antivenin. Because of the great length of the fangs, a dose of venom can be delivered deep into tissue full of blood vessels.

Symptoms

The typical bite of a Gaboon viper turns the skin near the bite a red-violet color. Swelling may appear all over the body as well as at the site of the wound. This may be accompanied by cold sweating, internal bleeding, depressed heart action, blood in the urine, and extreme dif-

Gaboon Viper

A gaboon viper can easily bite all the way through a human foot or ankle.

ficulty in breathing. Because of the great quantity of blood that may infiltrate the tissues around the bite, there may be permanent damage to a limb. Tissue death and gangrenous infection may be extensive and difficult to treat.

Treatment

The Pasteur Institute manufactures an antivenin for *Bitis gabonica* that should be administered as soon as possible. If there has been great blood loss, the victim may require a transfusion. If the heartbeat is irregular or weak, heart medication may be required.

GILA MONSTER

HOW IT GETS PEOPLE

Heloderma suspectum

HABITAT

CLIMATIC ZONE

CLIMATIC ZONE

RATING

Who would not be terrified of something with the English name *monster* and the Latin species name *suspectum*? This reptile has also been called "the most repulsive creature alive." The Gila monster and its cousin "south-of-the-border," the Mexican beaded lizard, are the only known venomous lizards.

Nocturnal, the Gila monster moves very slowly and clumsily, becoming more agile as the night progresses and returning once again to its sluggish state before dawn. Students of Gila monsters in the Sonoran Desert along the Colorado River report that for as much as 98 percent of the year, the surface of the desert is too hot or too cold for these creatures; they spend most of this time in their burrows, where they consume, at a very low metabolic rate, the fat reserves they have stored up, mostly in their tails.

Gila Monster

In its frisky periods, the Gila monster can move quite quickly, both on land and in water. Seizing live prey with its powerful jaws, the Gila monster rolls on its back and chews with its grooved teeth, forcing its venom into its victim. The naturalist Ernest R. Tinkham noted, "On the first bite of an enraged Gila monster, approximately 35 envenomed teeth of both lower and upper jaws are able to introduce a lethal dose of poison into a victim." Its jaws are so strong that it can hold its grip for a full 10 to 15 minutes. A baby Gila monster once caught Dr. Tinkham with just a few teeth, and he had to be hospitalized for a week. Small animals die very quickly from Gila monster venom, but in humans its effects vary considerably, with only about one-third of all bites being fatal.

One hunter was fatally bitten when he blindly brushed from his chest a Gila monster that had crawled on top of him in his sleep. The Gila monster clamped down on the hunter's wrist, and he died a few hours later. Two fatalities occurred when the victims placed Gila monsters *inside* their shirts. As with many reptile envenomizations, some Gila monster victims were drunk at the time and openly tempting fate. An intoxicated military officer in the southwestern United States placed a

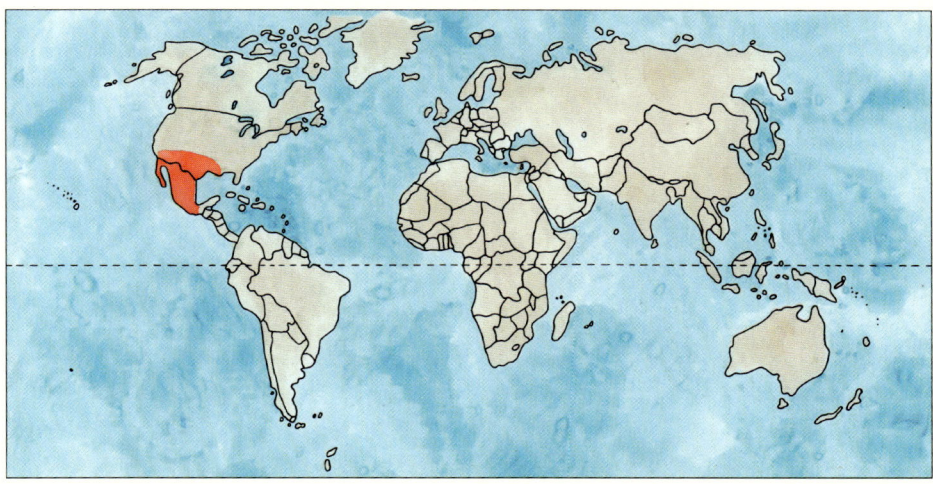

Dangerous Reptilian Creatures

Gila monster on a table to see if he could get his finger in and out of the monster's mouth before being bitten. The officer could not, but luckily did not suffer serious envenomization. Bogert and Martin report that another victim, who "was so drunk he wanted to eat up the earth," grabbed a Gila monster, was bitten at once, and died a short time later. As with many encounters with the natural world, lack of common sense seems to cause more injuries than anything else.

Name/Description
The Gila monster, or *Heloderma suspectum*, named after the Gila River in Arizona, is also known as the beaded or venomous lizard. Its cousin, the only other existing venomous lizard, is the Mexican beaded lizard, or *Heloderma horridum*. The Gila monster grows to two feet in length. Usually sluggish, the Gila monster has a formidable and heavy body, a massive head, tiny legs, and a short, stout tail used to store fat for periods when food is in short supply. Brightly colored, beadlike scales form gaudy patterns on its body. It uses its long, thick, forked tongue to taste the air and locate eggs, birds, and small mammals. The Gila monster seeks shelter under rocks or in burrows, which it often takes over from other animals. Its venom is located in glands outside the lower jaw. With a bulldoglike grip, it bites and chews its victims, forcing venom into the wound.

Toxicology
Heloderma venom contains serotonin, a powerful pain producer that also causes an elevation in blood pressure.

Symptoms
The bite of a Gila monster usually produces a large wound, which begins bleeding profusely very soon after the attack. There is immediate and often extreme pain, followed by sweating, swelling, weakness, an "unbearable" ringing in the ears, fever, nausea, vomiting, faintness, and

Gila Monster

Gila monsters chew on their victims, repeatedly poisoning prey with each bite of their venomous teeth.

emotional instability. The swelling spreads rapidly, and the skin may turn red or blue and become very sensitive to light. With severe envenomization there may be difficulty breathing, shock, and cardiac failure. Death occurs in about 33 percent of cases. Those most susceptible are children. See Bites, Gorings, Maulings, and Shock, page 121.

Treatment
Clean the wound and keep the victim quiet and still while you seek medical aid. Do not give alcohol or stimulants such as coffee. The wound should be treated by broad–spectrum antibiotics. There is an antivenin available in Arizona.

Prevention
- The Gila monster is shy by nature and will not attack a human being unless provoked, so the best prevention is to avoid handling these lizards.

GUINEA WORM

HOW IT GETS PEOPLE

Dracunculus medinensis

HABITAT

CLIMATIC ZONE

RATING

The Guinea worm was first mentioned in the Bible as the "fiery serpent" the Israelites encountered when wandering in the wilderness. Since that time, many generations of people in the Middle East, Africa, and Asia have suffered from dracunculiasis, an ulcerous infection caused by the little parasitic Guinea worm. Now affecting at least 50 million people, this crippling disease plagues African subsistence farmers wherever water supplies are contaminated by the cyclops, a water flea that carries the Guinea worm. Intent on farming during the brief rainy season, which is also the season for Guinea worm transmission, farmers are reluctant to take the time to boil their drinking water, even if they have a proper fireproof receptacle and the firewood to do so.

Guinea Worm

Once inside the human body, the mature female Guinea worm works her way to the skin, where she creates an unsightly ulcer before dying. To remove the worm's decaying body, Africans still use an archaic method that has remained basically unchanged for the last 2,000 years. As the dead female's body is very delicate, it must be extracted very slowly and carefully. This is accomplished by daily winding a tiny bit of the worm's long body around a twig that remains bound to the affected limb until the whole process is complete, which may take up to a month.

This disabling disease is surely one of the most revolting known, but in poor countries its effects are especially devastating. It can keep the subsistence farmer confined to his hut for the crucial period when he needs to cultivate his land to provide food for his family for the coming year.

Name/Description

The Guinea worm, also known as the Medina worm (*Dracunculus medinensis*), is a slender nematode, a worm with a long, cylindrical, unsegmented body. It grows to a length between 24 and 40 inches. Its indirect life cycle

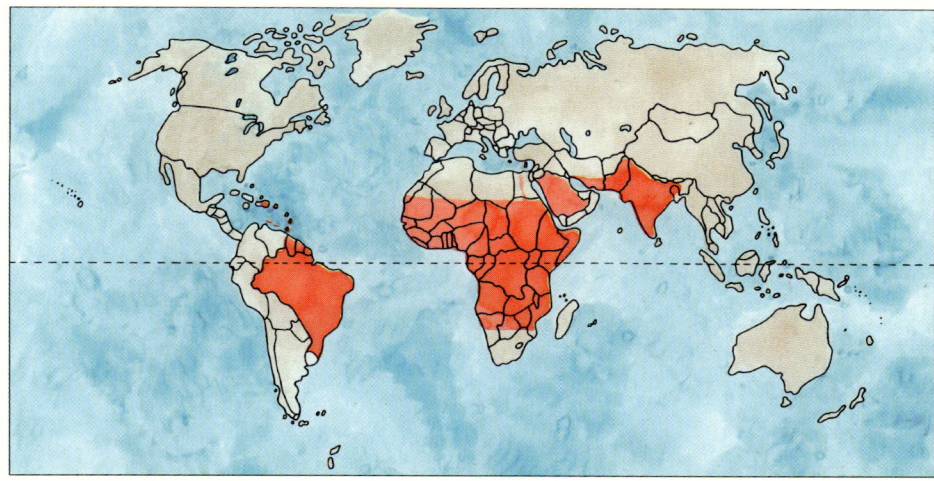

Dangerous Reptilian Creatures

depends upon a minute, shrimplike water flea that acts as an intermediate host. In humans, this water flea causes an ulcerous disease called dracunculiasis.

Infection
When they reach fresh water, Guinea worm larvae may be swallowed by water fleas. They will mature inside the fleas, and after four weeks they are ready to infect human beings. When the fleas are ingested by humans—usually through drinking water—up to one million larvae are released into the victim's digestive tract. The larvae then burrow through the intestinal wall and migrate to the tissue just below the skin, where the female matures in 9 to 12 months. The female, when mature, secretes a substance that causes an ulcer to form around her head near the skin, to which she applies her genital opening. When the ulcer comes in contact with water, millions of larvae are discharged.

Symptoms
There will be an intense itching and burning rash around the ulcer, accompanied by malaise, dizziness, diarrhea, and a slight fever. There may also be pain and swelling severe enough to immobilize the victim. Secondary infections often develop along the track of the worm, causing inflammation or abcesses of the skin. Multiple infections are common, with the worms coming out at different sites, one after another or several at one time.

Treatment
To prevent the dead worm's body from breaking below the skin and decaying, only about one-fifth of an inch of the worm's body should be wound out each day. As some worms are four feet long, this process could take weeks. Surgical removal is not recommended. Niridazole and

Guinea Worm

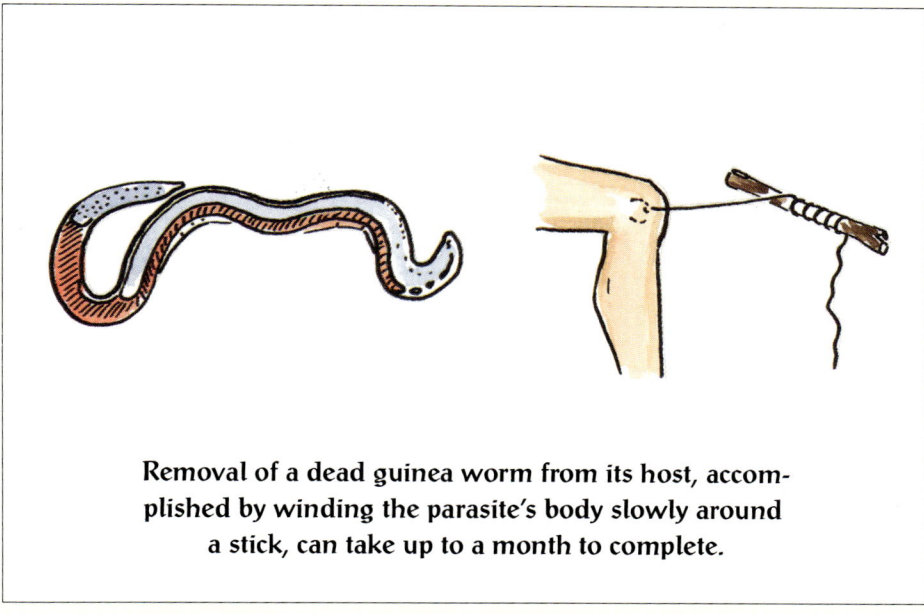

Removal of a dead guinea worm from its host, accomplished by winding the parasite's body slowly around a stick, can take up to a month to complete.

thiabendazole are of value in controlling dracunculiasis and lead to a rapid disappearance of symptoms. Ulcerated skin, even after successful removal of the worm, can easily become infected. Antibiotics and antitetanus serum may be given. Even if completely cured, one can easily become reinfected.

Prevention

- When traveling in tropical countries, only drink well–boiled or filtered water. Be careful of the water in which food is washed and prepared. The best filter is a new type with monofilament nylon gauge in a mesh size of 100 microns, which prevents passage of even the tiniest water fleas yet will not become clogged with silt or soil. The World Health Organization distributes these new filters in Upper Volta and India as part of a program to eradicate the disease.

HABU

HOW IT GETS PEOPLE

Genus Trimeresurus

HABITAT

HABITAT

HABITAT

HABITAT

CLIMATIC ZONE

CLIMATIC ZONE

RATING

Fortunately, the habu is confined to a tiny part of Asia and is found primarily on the Ryukyu Islands, a series of small islands strung like a chain from Japan southwest to Taiwan. Two of these islands, Amami and Okinawa, may well have the world's highest rate of snakebites, caused for the most part by the Okinawa habu, one of the largest of the Asian pit vipers. This slender-bodied snake is said to be highly irritable and will strike with lightning quickness if disturbed. The habu has specially jointed jaws that can rotate at an angle to each other, allowing the snake to get a better grip on its prey. The fangs are not grooved but feature

Habu

hollow canals through which the venom is transmitted, working very much like a hypodermic needle. The fangs are at the front of the mouth and leave two very distinctive puncture wounds at the point of entry. A habu bite will show other marks as well, made by the other teeth of the upper and lower jaws. At the end of World War II, many American soldiers returned home from the Pacific campaign bearing the scars of these distinctive puncture wounds. They were the lucky ones; they lived. The battle for Okinawa and other islands in the Ryukyu chain produced many victims of habu bites. One 20-year-old marine private was bitten twice while lying in some bushes, peering down on some Japanese soldiers moving below him. The marine thought he felt a twig poke him in the face and anxiously turned to see what it was. As he turned he was immediately struck a second time, just below the left eye, by a habu. He and nine other soldiers who were bitten received proper medical care and eventually returned to active duty.

Native agricultural workers on these islands have also suffered terribly from the habu. There have been so many victims, mostly men between the ages of 40 and 60, that the Japanese government began an

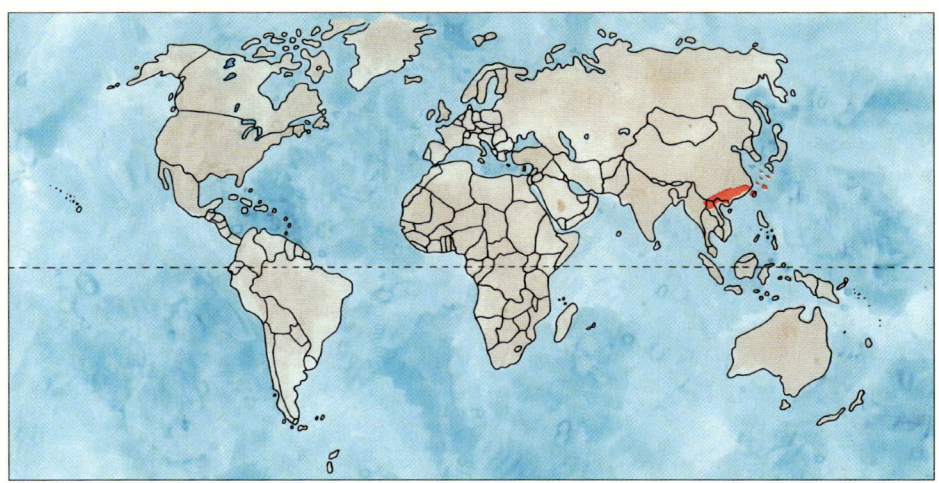

Dangerous Reptilian Creatures

extensive immunization program in the mid-1960s. In 1965 alone, more than 43,000 workers were immunized with habu toxoid. In the following three years, 168 of them were bitten. Five of the immunized victims developed gangrenous infections. Three suffered permanent disabilities, and two others died. The immunization campaign was judged useful but was by no means a guarantee against habu poisoning. One does not have to be working in a field to get bitten. One-third of all snakebites on the island of Taiwan occur inside people's houses.

Name/Description

There are four species of Asian habu, all lance-headed pit vipers of the genus *Trimeresurus*. Each has a large, flattened, triangular-shaped head that is much wider than its narrow neck. The eyes are rather small, and the pupils are elliptical. Their body shapes vary from cylindrical to slightly flattened, and the tails vary in length from about two and a half to six and a half feet. All four species are similar in appearance. The largest species is the Okinawa habu, or *Trimeresurus flavoviridis*, which is confined to the Ryukyu Islands and grows to about five feet, though a specimen six and a half feet long has been measured. Its distinctive color pattern is usually a light brown or olive green with blotches of dark green or brown, edged with yellow, along its back. These dorsal blotches often fuse to form a stripe that may or may not run the entire length of the body. The Sakishima habu, *T. elegans*, is found on the southern Ryukyu Islands, and while it resembles the Okinawa habu, it is much smaller. The himehabu, *T. okinavenis*, occupies the same range as the Okinawa habu, but this species is a short-bodied snake growing to a maximum of two and a half feet, and its coloration is usually dull brown with indistinct dorsal blotches. The Chinese habu, *T. mucrosquamatus*, is very similar in habits and appearance to the other habus and is found in south China, Taiwan, and throughout Southeast Asia as far west as Myanmar. It is usually found on farmland or near human dwellings. Its venomous fangs can be more than half an inch long. All habus are fertile

Habu

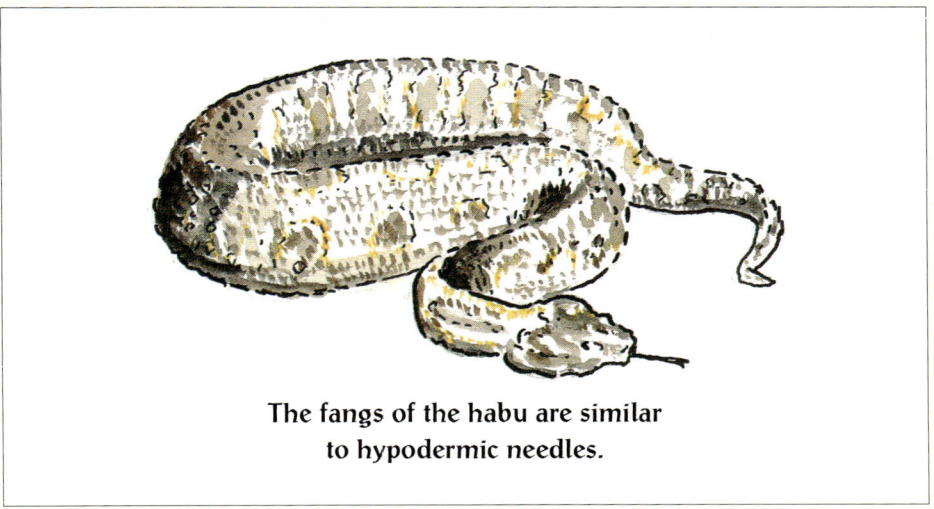

The fangs of the habu are similar to hypodermic needles.

breeders and usually feed on a variety of small vertebrates, particularly mice and rats.

Toxicology
Habu venom is hemotoxic, that is, it can destroy erythrocytes, the red blood corpuscles that carry oxygen to the body tissues.

Symptoms
The habu bite will produce symptoms of severe blood poisoning, such as burning pain, inflamed swellings, discoloration of the skin, a sudden drop in blood pressure, internal bleeding, and the formation of an abscess at the site of the bite. Death is due to heart failure.

Treatment
For first aid measures and medical treatment, see Snakebites, page 116.

KOMODO DRAGON

HOW IT GETS PEOPLE

Varanus komodoensis

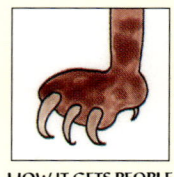
HOW IT GETS PEOPLE

HABITAT

HABITAT

HABITAT

HABITAT

CLIMATIC ZONE

RATING

The Komodo dragon is indeed one of the last of the giant reptiles, a descendant of dinosaurs that has survived for millions of years in the jungles of three tiny Indonesian islands. Weighing 300 pounds, with supple scales wrinkling its muscular body, it has claws that can shred a deer or rip a wild boar to pieces. Stalking prey by scent alone, it flicks its forked tongue over the ground like a snake.

Komodo Dragon

Southeast Asia abounds with legends about dragons and monsters, and the first rumors of this "terrestrial crocodile" had all the classic ingredients—"ferocious prehistoric beasts marooned on remote, uninhabited islands which no white man had seen before and which the natives regarded as primeval spirits." It was too good to be true. The rumors were so enticing that by 1910 the director of the Botanical Gardens at Buitenzorg (now Bogor), Java, Major P. A. Ouwens, asked the official responsible for the island to investigate. Governor Van Steyn van Hensbroek landed on the island of Komodo in 1912. There he encountered some people who described all sorts of fantastic run-ins with the dragons and led the governor to a dragon cave. There Van Steyn shot a small specimen, about seven feet long, the skin of which he sent with a photograph to Ouwens. Later, another party managed to capture two live Komodo dragons for the Buitenzorg Gardens.

Interest in these exotic creatures waned during World War I, but after the war, a former German prince and explorer, Duke Adolf Friedrich von Mecklenburg, shot four giant dragons and revived interest in these creatures. One dragon aficionado, Douglas Burden, trustee of the

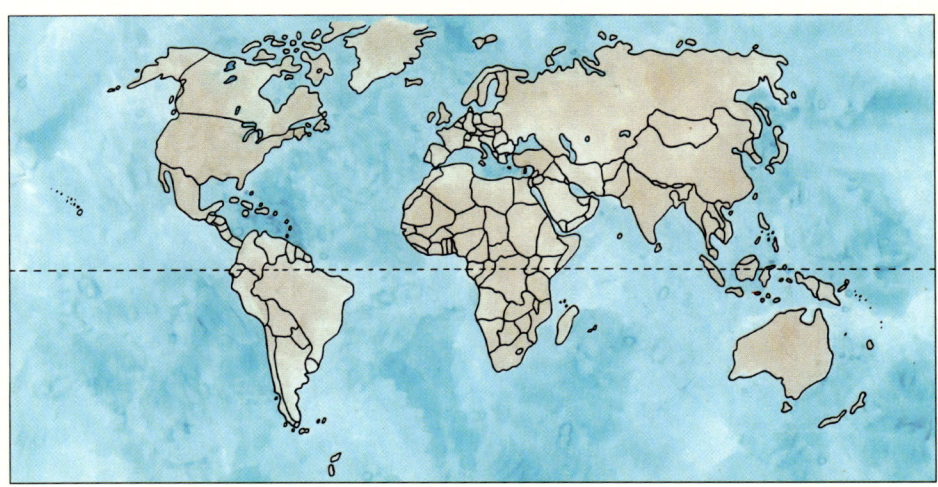

Dangerous Reptilian Creatures

American Museum of Natural History in New York City, immediately outfitted an expedition and headed to Komodo. Though he caught and shot a dozen specimens, he was exaggerating somewhat in his book *Dragon Lizards of Komodo* when he described the habitat of the Komodo dragon as "a place of terror, where death lurks on every hand. With their dragon's head, yellow, forked tongue and powerful claws they looked like survivors from the dim and distant past; they were soon among the favorite animals of zoo-goers." Soon thereafter, Komodo dragons became a favorite of European zoos.

Name/Description

The Komodo dragon (*Varanus komodoensis*) of the monitor lizard family is the world's largest living lizard. It weighs about 300 pounds and grows to more than 10 feet in length. It has a thick tail that is often as long as its body. The limbs are well developed, and the claws are talonlike. Its teeth are long and jagged. Its scales are gray-black. The Komodo dragon moves quickly and is a good swimmer and climber. It tends to live near water. Active during the day, it preys on wild boar, small deer, and pigs.

Injury

Komodo dragons can inflict appalling wounds that can become seriously, even fatally, infected. Their teeth and jaws are so powerful that they can bring down a water buffalo by severing the tendons of its hind legs, and their sharp claws are adept at shredding flesh. The resulting wounds can easily become infected by the bacteria in the decomposed flesh of previous victims lodged in the dragon's paws and teeth. Komodo dragons like to burrow into their victims' guts to feast and so are often covered with slime, blood, and gristle. For symptoms and treatment, see Bites, Gorings, Maulings, and Shock, page 121.

Komodo Dragon

Komodo dragons prefer to enter the bodies of their larger prey in order to feast upon them from the inside.

KRAIT

HOW IT GETS PEOPLE

Genus Bungarus

RATING

HABITAT

HABITAT

HABITAT

CLIMATIC ZONE

CLIMATIC ZONE

To say that the krait is nocturnal, that is, active at night, is to tell only half the story, for this is one snake whose inactivity during the day borders on a form of hibernation. As the herpetologist R. Mell has written, "During the day one can hit it, torture it, stick it, beat it on its head, and even nail it to a board, and still the krait remains phlegmatic even to the point of being killed; to my knowledge no one has ever managed to get a sexually mature Bungarus to bite during the day." But

Krait

at night the krait is a killer. Its venom is so potent that even with immediate antivenin treatment in a superior hospital, there is only a 50–50 chance of survival. Colonel W. A. Noble, who has been a medical missionary in India for 41 years, says that the natives of Madras call the krait the "seven-stepper" because they believe that, if bitten, a person can only take seven steps before dying.

The mortality rate for krait bites is high—much higher than that for cobra bites. Though they are not aggressive, when they do bite, they will clamp down with their strong jaws and hang on tenaciously, chewing their victim to inject more venom. The venom of some species, such as the Javan krait (*B. javanicus*), is incredibly toxic. A father and son were bitten in quick succession by the same snake in Yunnan province, China. Both died very soon afterward.

Dr. Norman Cheevers, an authority on medical jurisprudence in India, tells of a triple homicide involving a krait. Two snake charmers were instructing their four apprentices and claimed that if the apprentices would allow themselves to be bitten by a krait, their teachers could cure them with their magic powers. "They produced a krait about three

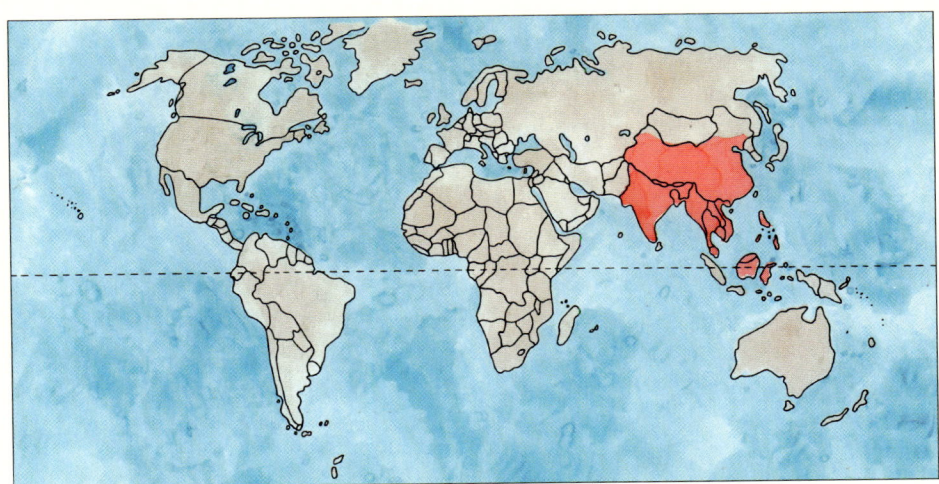

Dangerous Reptilian Creatures

feet long and placed it in front of the four men. . . . At first the snake did not bite, but when Poonai struck it with a cane, it immediately bit Titroo. After this, in the same manner, the snake was made to bite Menghon and Jikree, and lastly Etwaree. Titroo died half an hour before daybreak. Menghon and Jikree appeared to be well after Titroo's death, but both died at mid–day. . . . Etwaree became seriously ill but recovered." The two snake charmers were sentenced to five year's imprisonment.

Name/Description

Nocturnal, kraits of the genus *Bungarus* burrow underground during the day and come out at night to feed on small mammals, lizards, fish, and other snakes. Averaging between three and four feet in length, they have fangs in the front of their mouth, and when they bite they chew to increase the quantity of venom injected. Cobralike, they are shy and reclusive and will only bite when they are provoked at night. Their name comes from the Hindi word *karait*.

Toxicology

The potency of krait venom varies with the species and its geographical location, but some of its toxic compounds are cholinesterase and protease, with other enzymes present.

Symptoms

The bite of the krait is virtually painless, and 3 to 5 hours—and sometimes up to 12 hours—will pass before symptoms develop. These will include headache, drooping of the eyelids, abdominal pain, weakness, a staggering gait, blurred vision, difficulty in swallowing, excessive salivation, stiffness of the jaws, coma, and breathing problems. Death usually comes from cardiac failure.

Krait

In India, the krait is nicknamed the "seven-stepper";
it is said that human victims of its venomous bite
can take only seven steps before dying.

Treatment
An antivenin for krait poisoning is available.

Prevention
- Be careful at night in krait-infested areas and be especially careful in areas where there are lots of rodents. Kraits will enter houses and even go into cities in search of mice and rats. See Snakebites, page 116.

LAND LEECH

HOW IT GETS PEOPLE

Haemadipsidae

CLIMATIC ZONE

HABITAT

HABITAT

HABITAT

RATING

The leech has been sucking human blood for ages. Its hosts have been either unknowing and unwilling victims or the patients of physicians who practiced the ancient art of bloodletting. The idea was to reduce fever and other symptoms of illness by lowering blood pressure, and it worked, until the patient died. George IV's daughter, Princess Charlotte, died from overbleeding during childbirth, thus leaving the English throne open for Queen Victoria. So common was the use of leeches by early physicians that the Old English synonym for doctor was "leech," and "leechcraft" meant the art of healing.

Leeches are now being used in the reattachment of severed fingers, toes, and ears. Microsurgery can reconnect arteries that send blood to the extremities, but sometimes not the veins that carry it back. After surgery, leeches are attached to the amputated part of the limb to prevent blood congestion until the circulatory system mends.

Land Leech

Though the land leech is much smaller and less of a bloodsucker than its aquatic cousin, it attacks in such numbers that the victim's loss of blood can be quite severe. A missionary, S. Langdon, whose garden in Sri Lanka was infested with innumerable tropical pests, wrote: "You will find the grass of my little park too full of life to afford pleasant walking. A few steps on the green carpet will make you acquainted, in all probability, with our notorious land leeches. . . . You may think them scarcely worthy of attention, only about an inch long, and thin as needles; but by the time they have been in your stocking—and they have most insinuating ways—for a quarter of an hour, you will realize that they are capable of wonderful development, and enlargement. . . . In some of our jungles they swarm. During a walk . . . one day I actually plucked 25 of these ferocious little wretches from my legs."

The leech can live for up to nine months on a single meal. Indeed, naturalist R. Lotz says that the leech, which is the only creature in the animal kingdom that appears not to suffer from hunger, would make the very best astronaut for long-term space flights.

Land leeches often wait in low vegetation near game tracks or paths, waiting for large, warm-blooded animals to come along. When a host

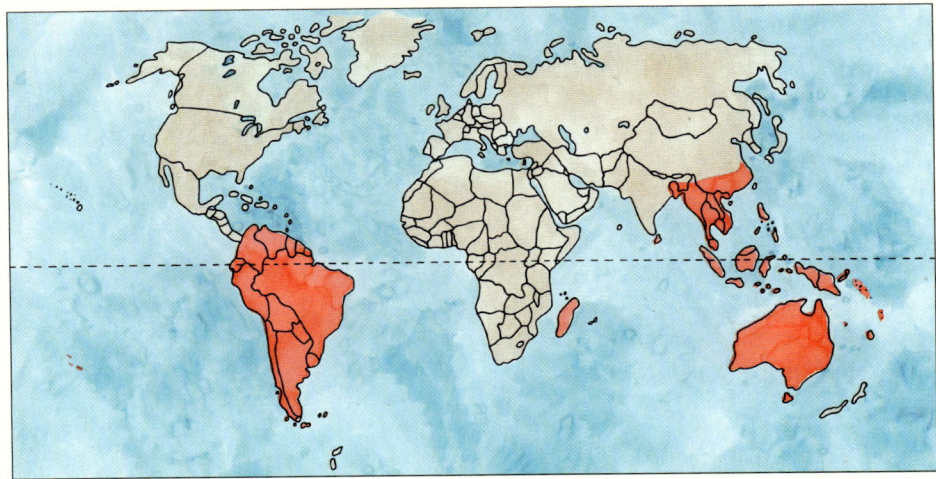

Dangerous Reptilian Creatures

passes by, they attach themselves to it with their anterior and posterior suckers, which they are able to do with incredible speed and efficiency. They usually go for the lower legs and ankles. They can creep through the smallest holes in protective clothing and even laced-up boots. Leeches are able to draw in three times their own weight in blood at one meal. As they engorge themselves, they contract from a long, slender, wormlike shape into a plump, figlike form.

Name/Description

The land leech is a bloodsucking worm of the family Haemadipsidae. Usually no more than one and one-quarter inches long, the leech has a flattened body with 30 to 33 segments, an anterior sucker around the mouth opening, and a posterior sucker. The midgut has many lateral pockets, which can hold large quantities of blood. All leeches are hermaphroditic, that is, bisexual, with a pair of ovaries and several pairs of testes. Unlike other annelids, or segmented worms, leeches have no bristles projecting from their body segments. To suck blood, they press their jaws against the skin, cutting through it like a circular saw, and leave a wound that looks like a jagged star.

Injury

The host's blood is sucked out by the muscular action of the leech's pharynx. From the pharynx, the blood enters the esophagus and goes into the crop, a large pouch with many branching pairs of smaller sacs. Inside the crop, water is removed from the blood. The remaining blood cells are stored in the crop, to be slowly digested by the leech. A meal usually consists of 10 to 15 milliliters of blood, and often after the leech drops off its host, another 20 to 50 milliliters will flow from the wound. See Bites, Gorings, Maulings, and Shock, page 121.

Symptoms

The victim usually does not feel anything while under attack, perhaps only noticing the dripping blood. The greatest danger lies in secondary

Land Leech

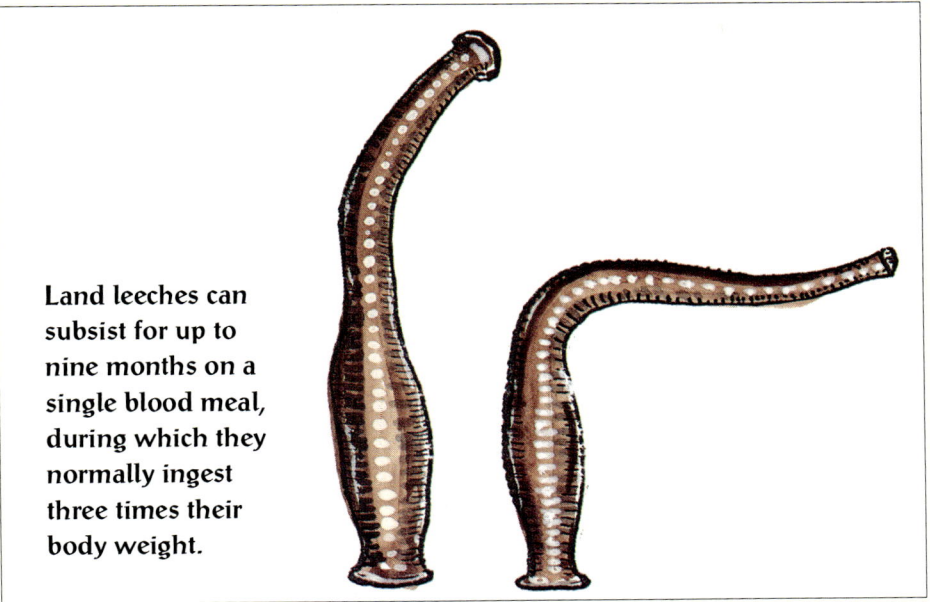

Land leeches can subsist for up to nine months on a single blood meal, during which they normally ingest three times their body weight.

infections, which may develop from improperly cleaned wounds. If the loss of blood is severe the victim may become weak.

Treatment
Remove the leech by applying salt, alcohol, or vinegar, or by touching the leech with a lighted match or burning cigarette. Do not try to pull it off or the mouth parts may remain in the wound and become infected. Wash the affected area well with soap and water, and then apply antiseptic.

Prevention
- Smother socks, boots, and trousers with any ointment containing dibu–typhalate or n–diethylmetatoluamide. Coarse tobacco rolled into the tops of socks and kept moist is also said to be an effective leech deterrent.

NEOTROPICAL TOAD

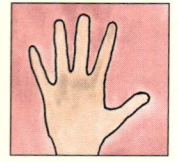
HOW IT GETS PEOPLE

Genus Bufo

HOW IT GETS PEOPLE

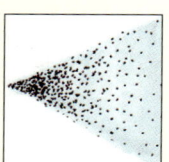
HOW IT GETS PEOPLE

HABITAT

HABITAT

HABITAT

CLIMATIC ZONE

CLIMATIC ZONE

RATING

For many centuries toads have been part of the dark side of human legend and history. They were an essential ingredient of the witches' "hell-broth" in Shakespeare's *Macbeth*. King John of England was rumored to have been poisoned by a friar who placed a toad in his cup of wine.

Slimy, venomous, Neotropical toads are not exactly what anyone, least of all a fairy princess, would want to kiss. But, says University of Arizona toxicologist Michael Hitt, "Children often try to kiss, eat, or mouth toads." In the British medical journal *Lancet*, Hitt wrote of a

Neotropical Toad

five-year-old boy who "had been seen placing one of his toads in his mouth. Within ten minutes of this action, he approached his mother, salivating profusely, and told her he felt sick." The toad's poison had gone straight to the boy's nervous system, causing partial paralysis, slurred speech, and seizures.

Indigenous to Central and South America, Neotropical toads were introduced into the West Indies and several other islands to feed on and eradicate crop-destroying insects on sugar plantations. Neotropical toads first appeared in the southern United States in the 1950s, when several of them hopped away from a broken crate at Miami International Airport.

Neotropical toads have bizarre sexual practices. The male toad will clamber onto a female's back and clasp strongly, sometimes holding on for days. With many males fiercely competing for eligible females, as many as 12 suitors may try to mount a female at the same time. Their weight may suffocate her, and unrelenting, the males may still hang on for several days as her body decomposes beneath them. If the males cannot find any females, they will attempt to mate with anything in sight—sticks, water lilies, and even goldfish.

Dangerous Reptilian Creatures

The frogs and toads of the tropical forests have evolved highly toxic skin secretions to let their predators know they can be quite dangerous to eat. For centuries, the Indians of South America have used the poisonous secretions of Neotropical toads on their darts and arrowheads. Even the toads' eggs are highly poisonous. Nor do you have to touch or ingest Neotropical toads or their eggs to be poisoned; you can merely be looking at one. One species of Neotropical toad can squirt its poison as far as a foot away.

Name/Description

Neotropical toads—about 18 species of the genus *Bufo*—also known as giant toads, marine toads, or aga toads, are the world's largest toads. They are especially equipped for survival in relatively dry habitats. Greenish brown, rough-skinned amphibians, Neotropical toads are characterized by horizontal pupils and enlarged poison glands located behind the eyes. Neotropical toads usually measure about six to eight inches in length and weigh about a pound. One *Bufo marinus*, a resident of the Black Park Zoo in Des Moines, Iowa, aptly named Totally Awesome, measured nine and a half inches and weighed over five pounds.

Though its main source of food is insects, occasionally the Neotropical toad eats plant material in such large quantities that it bloats up like a ball. Able to pass urine with considerable force, some toads can spray it as far as one yard away. Their voice is a low-pitched trill.

Toxicology

The toad's toxins, consisting of some two dozen potent chemicals, are located in the large parotid glands extending from the back of the head down the sides of the body and are secreted through the toad's skin when the creature is irritated or threatened. The toxic compounds include secretions called bufagin and bufotenine. These toxins can cause death by disrupting normal heart rhythms.

Neotropical Toad

Even glancing at a neotropical toad can be fatal, as they can spray a poisonous substance at victims over a foot away.

Symptoms
Handling of some species will cause stinging, burning, and then numbing sensations, possibly followed by inflammation of the skin. If the victim has attempted to eat the toad or ingest some of its toxins, symptoms will include nausea, vomiting, numbness of the mouth and tongue, and tightness in the chest. In acute cases there may be convulsions, salivation, and seizures, followed by death.

Treatment
Immediately wash the affected area. If there are any cuts or open sores, apply an antiseptic. If the poisoning is internal, give syrup of ipecac to induce vomiting. Activated charcoal may be ingested to absorb the toxins.

Prevention
- The best preventive measure is to never kiss or even touch strange toads.

POISON FROGS

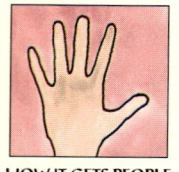
HOW IT GETS PEOPLE

Genera Physalaemus, Dendrobates, Rana, Hyla, and Phyllobates

HOW IT GETS PEOPLE

HABITAT

HABITAT

HABITAT

CLIMATIC ZONE

RATING

Doris Cochran, a leading authority on poison frogs and toads, calls the poison frogs of the Dendrobatidae family "the Borgia of the anurans." According to Hickman, "The poisons of the dendrobatid frogs are the most lethal secretions known, drop for drop more poisonous even than the venoms of sea snakes or any of the most poisonous arachnids." The venom of the Colombian arrow-poison frog (*Phyllobates aurotaenia*) may be "the most active cardiotoxin known."

It does not seem possible that something so tiny could be so deadly. The Kokoi arrow-poison frogs (*Phyllobates bicolor*) are said to be "handsome little creatures," only three-fourths of an inch long and weighing

Poison Frogs

only about one-third of an ounce. They secrete bactrachotoxin, one ounce of which is enough to kill 2,500,000 people.

The Kokoi Indians of Colombia locate and capture these minute creatures by imitating the frogs' peeping. They pierce the frogs through the mouth and body with a sliver of wood and roast them over a fire. The heat contracts the skin, forcing the poison out of the glands just under the skin. The poison is collected and stored in a vessel, where it undergoes a fermentation process. Darts and arrowheads are then dipped in the poison and used when hunting to bring down swift prey, such as monkeys or birds, inflicting almost instant paralysis and death.

Said to be somewhat like curare—a poison extracted from a tropical vine—this frog's poison affects the muscles as well as the central nervous system. Like curare, it is usually harmless when taken orally, but if there is even a tiny scratch in the mouth or an ulcer in the digestive tract, the person ingesting this substance could become dangerously ill. Thus, when the Cholos, another South American tribe, cut out the arrow from an animal, they also remove a small piece of meat from around the wound as a precaution.

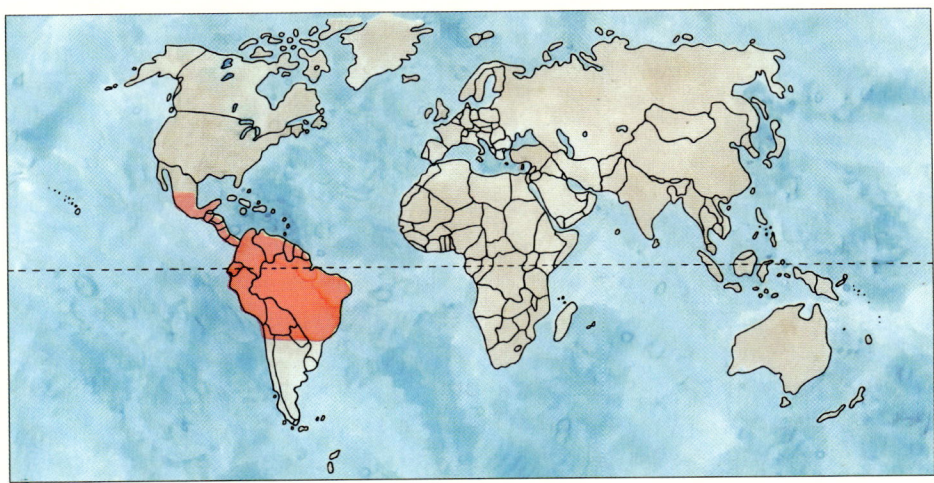

Dangerous Reptilian Creatures

Behaviorally, poison frogs are among the most intriguing of frogs. They are very territorial. Each territory is marked by a prominent object, such as a large rock. The frog will produce an incessant chirping noise if that area is approached by another frog. Often these frogs will stage ritualized combat involving both males and females and sometimes even the young. When the tadpoles are born, usually in a pool of water inside a bromeliad plant up in the trees, the young will wiggle onto the father's back, where they arrange themselves in two rows. The father will then carry them to deeper water, where he will deposit them to fend for themselves.

Name/Description

Poison frogs are found in the New World tropics, that is, the rain forests of South and Central America. Usually no more than one to two inches in length, they are slender and exhibit extraordinary color patterns. The basic color is a dark one, overlaid with spots and streaks of vivid pink, yellow, green, red, or orange. These bright colors warn predators to stay away. The poison glands are usually clustered on the sides of the head and shoulders. When the frog is threatened, it secretes a thick, creamy, toxic substance. Individual species are very difficult to distinguish, and even different populations of the same species can vary in size and color.

Toxicology

The toxins of poison frogs are complex combinations of chemical compounds such as histamine, bufotenine, physalaemin, serotonin, steroidal alkaloids, and other substances, all of which act on the nervous system. Sometimes the only certain way to identify a species is to analyze the specific composition of its poison. The effects of the toxins seem almost irreversible. One of the principle toxic substances of the frogs of the genera Hyla and Phyllobates is bactrachotoxin, 25 times more potent than curare and 500 times more potent than cyanide.

Poison Frogs

Researchers claim that the venom of the poisonous toad is one of the most lethal secretions in the natural world.

Symptoms
Contact of poisonous secretions with the skin produces a burning sensation, and on some individuals a rash. In the eye, these poisons may produce a severe inflammatory reaction. A contaminated hand rubbed against the nose will produce swollen, runny, nasal mucous membranes for two to three days. Swallowing the poison produces nausea, vomiting, and abdominal pain. If the toxin enters an open wound, there will be a feeling of general malaise. If the poisoning is severe, there may be convulsions, paralysis, and death.

Treatment
As quickly as possible, clean the skin of all toxic secretions. A soothing lotion such as calamine may help. If the poison was ingested, give syrup of ipecac and induce vomiting. There is no known antidote.

Prevention
- Do not play with frogs from the tropics or you may have to follow naturalist Charles Levy's suggestion for the only possible cure: "Try prayer."

RETICULATED PYTHON

HOW IT GETS PEOPLE

Python reticulatus

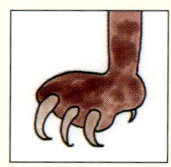
HOW IT GETS PEOPLE

HABITAT

HABITAT

CLIMATIC ZONE

RATING

For centuries, pythons have been venerated in Africa. In Dahomey, priestesses carried them in processions, and if anyone was caught killing a python he was shut up in his hut, which was then set afire with the offender inside. If he managed to escape, it was looked upon as a kind of divine intervention, and the culprit was set free. Each village in Dahomey kept a python as a "living god" in a circular clay temple. The snake was thought to control the water supply, the earth's productivity, and human fertility. Tribes on Mount Meru in Tanzania believe that a dying python spits out a gem just before it perishes. If they cannot find a gem near a dead python, the tribes accuse each other of stealing it. When the kings of Nigeria made treaties with England, the protection of pythons was written into the pacts. Once, a band of Africans got hold of a European who had killed a python inside his own house. The enraged natives tied the man's thumbs together, spit on him, and stripped him naked. The local colonial administrator thought it wiser to let the natives go unpunished. When the Portuguese brought slaves from Dahomey and Uganda to the Americas in the 18th century, python worship came

Reticulated Python

along. On the island of Haiti, the python cult formed the nucleus of the voodoo religion.

There are many accounts of animal handlers and snake charmers who have suffered rib injuries inflicted by these behemoths, especially during the 1920s and 1930s, when a snake show was part of every carnival and circus in America. Those who only suffer rib injuries are the lucky ones, as many attacks are fatal. The first properly recorded attack was of that of a 14-year-old Malaysian boy who, on the island of Salebabu in 1927, was killed and swallowed by a reticulated python approximately 14 feet long. Snakes can separate their upper jaws from their lower jaws so that their jaws are joined only by cartilage, enabling them to open their mouths very wide. A python more than 30 feet in length can open its mouth wider than most. Pythons in the Frankfurt Zoo have easily consumed animals weighing over 120 pounds, so that a small Malaysian boy may have seemed like an appetizer. Harder to swallow must have been the Portuguese sailor who, in 1973, vanished while on guard duty one night and whose body was said to have been "retrieved" from the stomach of a giant python. Herpetologist Arthur Loveridge reported the death of a young mother in Lake Victoria who

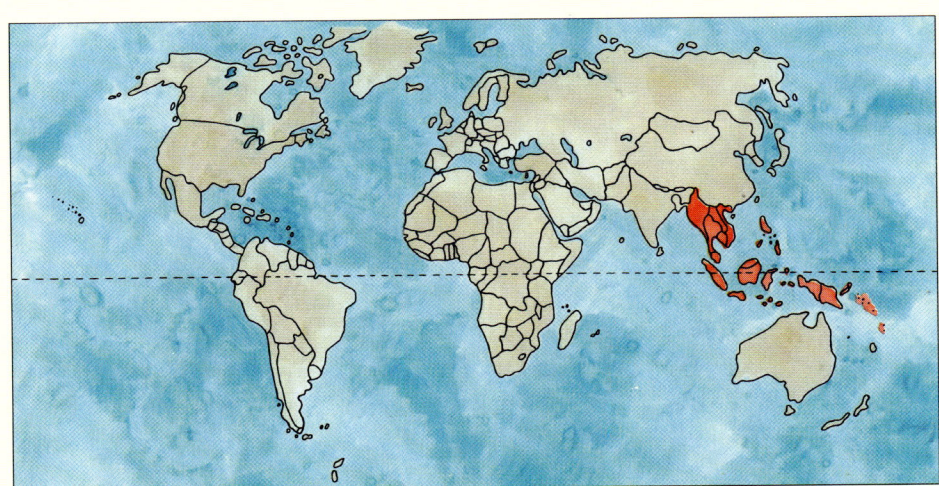

Dangerous Reptilian Creatures

was found still in the coils of a 14-foot python. But some victims do escape, as noted in this report from the *Pretoria News* of February 26, 1975: "A Durban gardener fought a life-and-death struggle with a huge python when it dropped on him from a tree and tried to squeeze him to death while he was cutting a hedge in Greenwood Park yesterday. . . . After five horrifying minutes, Mr. Ngurta managed to free himself from the snake by wriggling out of his overalls." Pythons have also been used as murder and torture weapons. Americans used pythons in Vietnam to make Vietcong prisoners and suspected sympathizers "more cooperative."

Name/Description

Pythons are the most familiar genus in the python subfamily Pythoninae. The reticulated python (*Python reticulatus*) reaches a length approaching 33 feet and can weigh up to 440 pounds. It vies with the anaconda for the title of the world's largest snake, although it is lighter and more slender than its South American counterpart. The python's intricate, reticulated skin pattern camouflages it well against the lights and shades of Southeast Asian rain forests. All pythons have heat-sensing pits located in their upper lips. They have about 100 teeth in their powerful jaws, but their bite is nonvenomous.

    A female python may have as many as 100 offspring at a time. After she lays her eggs, she will gently coil around them to keep them warm. Pythons hunt both day and night, and though they prefer warm-blooded prey such as small mammals and birds, they will also eat an occasional lizard. During the day their pupils constrict in the sunlight to form vertical slits, while at dusk they widen to look like cats' eyes. Pythons have poor vision but a good sense of smell. They are rather slow and move forward with a sort of glide, somewhat like an earthworm. Younger pythons shed their skin five to nine times a year; older pythons shed only four to seven times a year. Pythons are good swimmers, and in the water they will pump air into their bodies to help them float. In the wild, pythons may live from 40 to 50 years.

Reticulated Python

The reticulated python can weigh up to 440 pounds and measure an astonishing 33 feet.

Injury

Contrary to popular belief, pythons do not crush their victims. They slowly suffocate them. They coil their long bodies around their prey, and each time the victim exhales the python only needs to exert a slight increase in pressure to tighten its grip. Once a victim has lost consciousness, the python will release him, sniff him, and then eat him, beginning with the head, often while the victim is still alive.

Toxicology

Although the python's bite is nonvenomous, even a small bite usually causes copious bleeding, which suggests that there is an anticlotting agent in the python's saliva.

Symptoms

There will be pain in the area around the bite, and as noted, it may bleed profusely. Usually a python will seize an animal with its teeth in a quick, darting movement and then coil itself around its victim and start to suffocate it. The pressure often causes blood vessels to burst, especially in smaller prey.

Treatment

See Snakebites, page 116; and Bites, Gorings, Maulings, and Shock, page 121.

ROUGH-SKINNED NEWT

Taricha granulosa

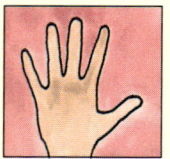
HOW IT GETS PEOPLE

HOW IT GETS PEOPLE

HABITAT

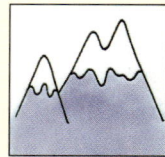
HABITAT

HABITAT

CLIMATIC ZONE

RATING

Considerable confusion exists about the terms salamander and newt, but they are really common rather than scientific names. The word *salamander* is frequently applied to all amphibians having a tail. The term *newt* originated in Europe and had a precise meaning, referring only to the European newts of the genus *Triturus*. The original *salamander* was a mythological reptile that was supposed to be able to endure fire.

Rough-skinned Newt

The rough-skinned newt is not interested in heat and prefers shaded ponds, lakes, streams, and their surrounding woodlands. Small, slow, and secretive, this poisonous newt and its cousin, the California newt, spend their days in cool, humid spots, constantly secreting mucus to keep the surface of their skin moist. Hardly characters out of Dante's *Inferno*!

The rough-skinned newt is able, like most amphibians with tails, to regenerate amputated parts such as a tail, leg, and even some parts of the head. These newts have some rather peculiar mating and defense postures. During the breeding season the male's skin temporarily becomes smooth, his tail becomes flattened, and his excretory vent swells. On the soles of his forefeet, horny growths called nuptial pads begin to develop, which help the male get a better grip on the female. On his back and tail a sort of crest will develop, which is usually brightly colored to attract females. The females, unlike other newts, lay their eggs one at a time, rather than in a mass, on submerged plants or debris.

When molested, the newt assumes a characteristic swayback defense pose, with its eyes closed, head and tail bent upward, limbs extended,

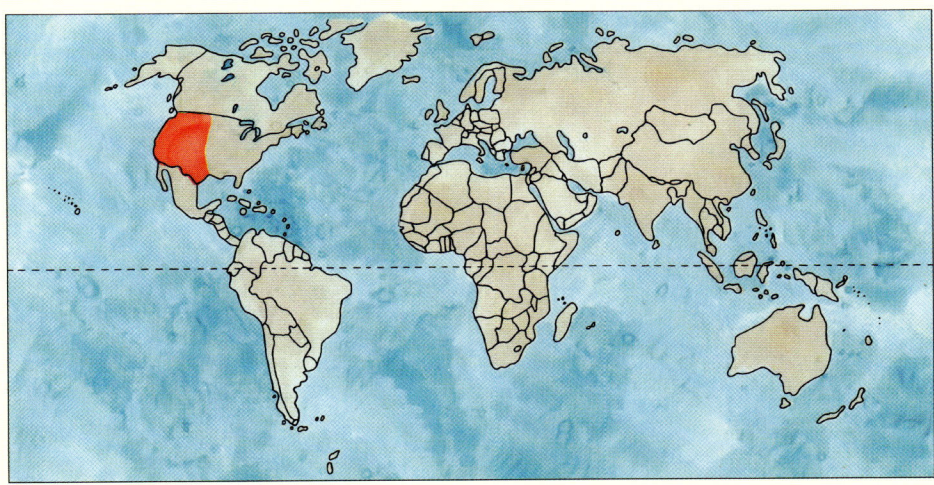

Dangerous Reptilian Creatures

and toes flexed. It is thought that the bright color of the newt's underside, being thus exposed, serves as a warning to would-be attackers. The highly poisonous toxin in their bodies is identical to the deadly tetrodotoxin of the puffer fish and keeps most sensible prey at bay. But it seems that foolish people will never learn. A few years ago, the *Journal of the American Medical Association* reported that a 21-year-old camper who was drunk swallowed an eight-inch rough-skinned newt and died eight hours later from cardiac arrest.

Name/Description

The rough-skinned newt, *Taricha granulosa*, is also known as the Oregon, or western, rough-skinned newt and has, like its cousin the California newt, warty skin, four clawless toes, and a tail that may be longer than its body. It has no external ear openings, and the teeth in the roof of its mouth are in a V-shaped arrangement. It grows from two and a half to five inches long. It has a dark, greenish brown back and a yellowish red underbelly. The adults are land dwellers, preferring humid woods, and return to the water only to breed. Voracious feeders, these newts detect their food by sight and smell, eating worms, slugs, snails, insects, aquatic larvae, small crustaceans, mollusks, and even frog eggs. The newt swims by swinging its tail, with the limbs usually held alongside the body. Its toxic secretions repel most of its enemies. The rough-skinned newt is distinguished from the California newt by its smaller eyes and dark-colored lower lids.

Toxicology

The embryos, skin, and eggs of adult newts contain a powerful poison, tetrodotoxin, that acts on the nervous system, interfering with the movement of sodium ions across cell membranes—a process essential for nerve cell function. The poison is a milky substance secreted from skin glands in the tail region, and one newt contains enough poison to kill a grown man.

Rough-skinned Newt

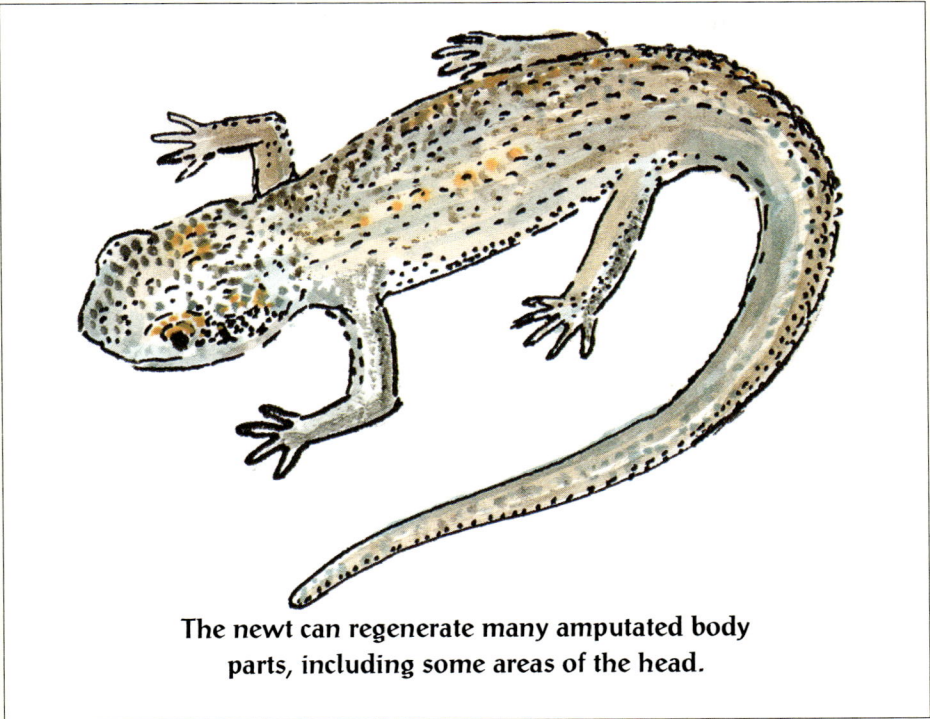

The newt can regenerate many amputated body parts, including some areas of the head.

Symptoms
There has been very little scientific analysis of newt poisoning, but victims have reported feeling a tingling in the lips, followed by a general numbness and weakness. Unconsciousness precedes death.

Treatment
If you touch a newt, wash your hands vigorously with soap and antiseptic, and do not put your hands near your mouth, eyes, or open cuts. If the toxin is ingested, give syrup of ipecac to induce vomiting. The victim may need help breathing. There is no known antidote to this toxin.

RUSSELL'S VIPER

HOW IT GETS PEOPLE

Vipera russellii

CLIMATIC ZONE

HABITAT

HABITAT

RATING

The Russell's viper has a reputation for being shy and slow moving, but on occasion it can display a savage disposition and strike with great agility, in spite of its heavy body. Its venom delivery system is highly efficient. The bite is quite deep and painful, and long fangs and highly articulated jaws allow the Russell's viper to bite almost anywhere on a body. Powerful muscles strongly compress the venom gland so that its contents are violently expelled into the wound at the moment of the bite and injected under pressure through hollow teeth. Fortunately for many, the strike of the Russell's viper is preceded by a loud hissing. Colonel Wall, an expert on the snakes of India, has said, "Anyone who hears them hiss does not forget it." Arthur Conan Doyle gave this viper's fearsome reputation a big boost when he chose this snake as the murder weapon in his Sherlock Holmes story *The Speckled Band*.

Russell's Viper

The Russell's viper can be encountered in the warmer regions of Asia and the Indian subcontinent, where it is a special threat to barefoot farm workers. As it has the unfortunate habit of lingering on footpaths and roadways and even entering homes in search of food, it can be a danger even in urban areas. The Russell's viper can be quite tenacious, and once it digs its fangs into its victim it will not let go easily. Once, in India, a dog was bitten and could not shake the viper off; it dragged the snake around for a half hour before succumbing to the poison. The Russell's viper is considered to be the most dangerous species of viper. Its highly toxic venom is slow acting but injected in great quantity. A single milking yields between 150 and 250 milligrams of venom, perhaps the largest amount of venom given off by any viper. Only 70 milligrams are needed to kill a human being. Death usually results from kidney failure or prolonged shock. The slow-acting quality of the venom, however, has been a blessing to many, including a Czechoslovakian scientist who was bitten while working in his laboratory. As he had no anitvenin, he sent a telegram to the East Berlin Zoo to ask for the serum. It was flown to Czechoslovakia in time to save the scientist's life. But one cannot count

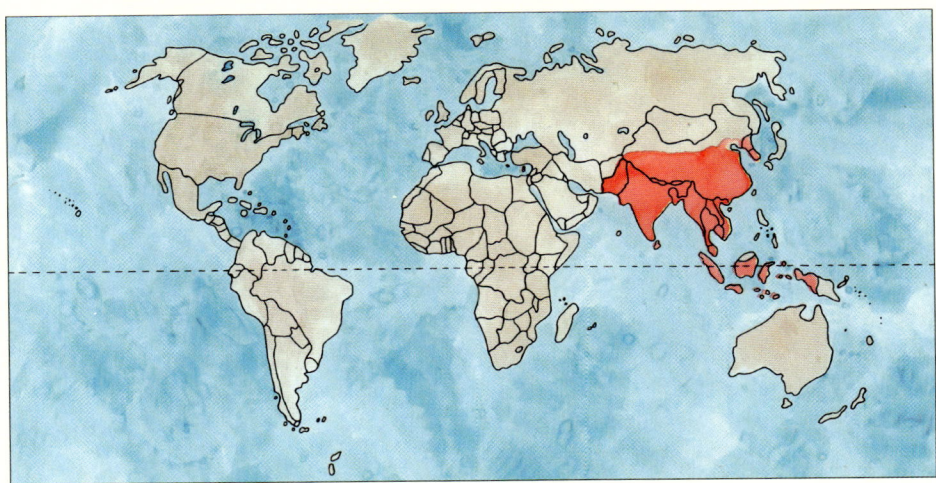

on such a delayed reaction if the bite penetrates a major blood vessel. One woman in Sri Lanka died within 15 minutes of being bitten by a Russell's viper that had "evidently struck a vein."

Name/Description

Said to be the most beautiful of vipers, the Russell's viper has a string of diamond patterns along its trunk. Each diamond is colored brown and bordered in black. The nocturnal Russell's viper is shy and lives in isolated places, but will go far afield in search of food. It can be found inhabiting climates from sea level to an altitude of 7,000 feet. Its fangs are longer than a cobra's, and its venom is more deadly. Like other members of the viper family, it has hollow fangs and an articulated upper jaw for better gripping, but it lacks heat sensors. It grows to a length of about five feet. Once it bites, it digs in powerfully and deeply with its oversized fangs. The female Russell's viper can give birth to as many as 60 young, each a foot long.

Toxicology

Russell's viper venom is slow acting. The principle toxic compounds are carboxypolypeptidase, cholinesterase, dipeptidase, lipase, lecithinase, and protease.

Symptoms

Symptoms include rapidly spreading edema and internal bleeding. The blood will not clot, and there may be bleeding from the gums, intestines, and urinary tract. The victim will also experience abdominal pain and vomiting. There will be loss of consciousness, a fall in blood pressure, circulatory failure, and shock before death.

Russell's Viper

Vipers have a tenacious bite; one dog, unable to shake off its attacker, dragged the viper around for half an hour before dying.

Treatment

An antivenin for Russell's viper is available. As the venom is so slow acting, one can live for two weeks and then still succumb to the poison. See Snakebites, page 116.

TAIPAN

HOW IT GETS PEOPLE

Oxyuranus scutellatus

CLIMATIC ZONE

HABITAT

HABITAT

RATING

With more than 360 venomous animals, Australia may seem a dangerous place. The deadly taipan is Australia's most poisonous snake. The taipan is very active and is capable of injecting an enormous dose of highly potent, neurotoxic venom.

When aroused, the taipan makes an alarming display, flattening its head and neck and raising part of its 12-foot-long body off the ground. It also raises its tail and waves it back and forth. It can strike with

Taipan

lightning speed. It almost always makes a series of rapid bites, and it may strike several times before the victim realizes what has happened. But even if a victim springs back after the first strike, he has already received the bulk of the taipan's venom. Without immediate antivenin, there is only about a 20 percent recovery rate, and even with immediate treatment, many people die. Taipans strike quickly, and taipan victims die quickly. A good-sized riding horse in Queensland, Australia, died only five minutes after being bitten, and humans have died in even less time. If you are bitten by a taipan far away from any possible medical treatment, how would you spend your last few minutes? Kevin C. Budden devoted his last moments to the further study of the serpent that had just fatally bitten him. Budden, a young museum collector, was gathering specimens for research purposes. He had just captured a taipan and was carrying it to his car when he was bitten on the thumb. Budden knew immediately that he was going to die, and very quickly. Nevertheless, he packed the snake safely away and made arrangements for it to be shipped directly to his laboratory for study. The specimen lived; the collector died.

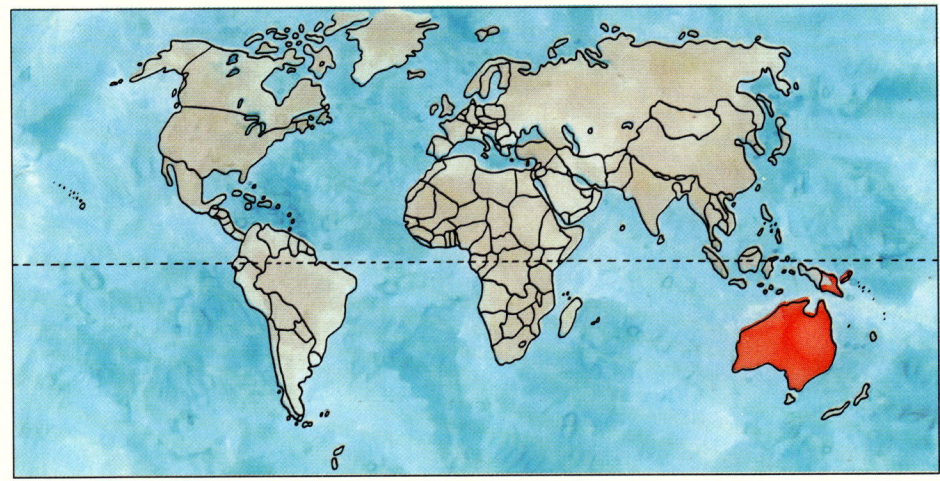

Dangerous Reptilian Creatures

Name/Description

The taipan (*Oxyuranus scutellatus*) is a large, highly dangerous snake of the Elapidae family found only in Australia and coastal New Guinea. Rather plain brown above and yellowish below, it has been measured at 12 feet and has very long fangs. Most active in the early morning and late evening, its chief prey consists of rats, and taipans are often found living in rat-infested quarters.

Toxicology

Taipan venom is essentially neurotoxic. Not only can it paralyze the central nervous system; it can also destroy red blood corpuscles. The principle toxic compounds are lecithinase and phospholipase.

Symptoms

Symptoms of taipan envenomization proceed rapidly and include nausea, vomiting, fainting, paralysis, sweating, drowsiness, staggering, slurred speech, difficulty in swallowing, drooping eyelids, and acute difficulty in breathing, eventually resulting in death.

Treatment

The recovery rate is quite possibly the lowest for all snakes. A victim has about a 20 percent chance of living without antivenin, which is available throughout Australia. Even with antivenin, many victims die. See also Snakebites, page 116.

Prevention

- Be especially careful around rats and rat holes.

Taipan

Taipan bite victims have the lowest recovery rate of all snakebite victims.

TIGER SNAKE

HOW IT GETS PEOPLE

Notechis scutatus

CLIMATIC ZONE

HABITAT

HABITAT

HABITAT

RATING

The two species of highly venomous tiger snakes are confined to Australia, Tasmania, and a few South Pacific islands. More than 3,000 Australians are hospitalized every year for snakebites, and the tiger snake takes its share. The most venomous land snake in the world, the tiger snake's venom is 4 times as toxic as that of the death adder, also found in Australia, 20 times more potent than that of the Asiatic cobra, and 100 times more deadly than the venom of Russell's viper of Southeast Asia. A fatal dose for an average 150-pound person is only one-five-thousandth of an ounce. In one study of 45 victims, 18 died—a fatality rate of 40 percent.

Tiger Snake

Although tiger snakes are active during both day and night, most fatalities occur when people accidentally step on them at night. The tiger snake is certainly one of the most aggressive reptiles to be found in Australia.

Name/Description

Only one species of tiger snake is currently recognized—the Australian tiger snake *Notechis scutatus*. The black tiger snake is not thought by most scientists to be a separate species, although herpetologist Eric Worrell believes that it is. The Australian tiger snake's coloration is variable and ranges from gray, olive, and brown to red, and some individuals may be very dark brown, almost black. Markings consist of narrow crossbands of yellow or creamy white. The black tiger snake is very dark brown or black, with light crossbands that are indistinct in many individuals. All tiger snakes eat a wide range of food, including frogs, small mammals, birds, and even other snakes.

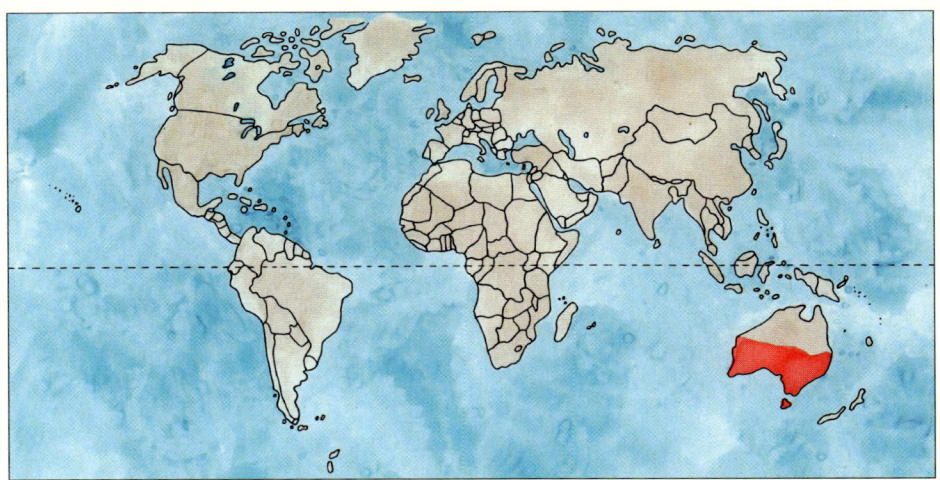

Dangerous Reptilian Creatures

The tiger snake grows to four or five feet in length, although one specimen, found on Chappell Island, measured eight feet. The head is relatively broad and flattened. Its eyes are of moderate size, and the pupils are round. There are usually nine scales on the crown of the head. The jaw contains three to five small teeth and two rather long fangs.

Symptoms

Pain, usually of minor intensity, may appear within the first 10 minutes after the bite, although in some cases it is not reported for 30 minutes or longer. Swelling usually appears two or three hours after the bite and tends to be limited to the area around the puncture wounds. The first serious symptom is an unusual drowsiness. The victim will become unable to raise his eyelids, and difficulty in speaking and swallowing may also occur. Blood pressure may fall, and the victim may vomit and sweat excessively. This will be followed by respiratory paralysis, which usually results in death in two to three hours.

Treatment

There is an effective antivenin now available for tiger snake envenomization. See Snakebites, page 116.

Tiger Snake

In Australia, home of the tiger snake, over 3,000 people are hospitalized annually for snakebites.

APPENDIX I:
Snakebites

Snake venom evolved to paralyze prey and to initiate the digestive process even as it kills. Each reptile's venom is adapted to and most effective against its natural prey. Unfortunately, many snake venoms have also proven highly effective against humans, and even now, after centuries of trying to find antidotes, we are far from the perfect cure. Many of the treatments used since World War II have now been abandoned as ineffective or even dangerous.

Antivenin, an antitoxin for snake venom, in spite of its sometimes painful and dangerous side effects, is the most widely used treatment available today. Antivenin is just one of the "Three A's" recommended by expert Roger A. Caras for poisonous reptile bites, the others being antitetanus and antibiotics. There are now several antivenins available, each one developed to counteract the venom of a particular group of snakes, such as the pit vipers, or an individual species, such as the coral snake. The only 100 percent infallible treatment seems to be that used by the Guanhibo Indians of South America—simply lop off the afflicted appendage!

Symptoms

Venomous snakes may bite and not inject any venom. For the symptoms and treatment of such wounds, see Bites, Gorings, Maulings, and Shock, page 121. Symptoms of snakebite envenomization are listed below according to the family group of the reptile.

Pit Viper Envenomization

The wound will swell within twenty minutes, followed by edema, the abnormal accumulation of fluid in the tissues. Untreated, edema may spread throughout the entire limb. The lymph nodes, usually located in the joints of the arms and legs, will become inflamed, enlarged, and tender. The skin and

Appendix I

body temperature may rise, although the patient may complain of chills. There may be skin discoloration, weakness, a rapid and weak pulse, fainting, sweating, nausea, and vomiting. The victim may go into shock or have serious difficulty breathing.

Viperid Envenomization

There will be local pain, swelling, edema, skin discoloration, and a small purplish blood spot on the skin near the wound. Bleeding from the wound and from the gums is common in severe Russell's viper envenomization. The blood may fail to clot. Severe poisoning is indicated by swelling along the upper arms or thighs, usually within two hours, or by bleeding.

Elapid Envenomization

Elapids include cobras, mambas, kraits, tiger snakes, coral snakes, and the African and Asian spitting snakes. Cobra bites are characterized by pain within 10 minutes, but the onset of swelling is slow. General symptoms include drowsiness, weakness, excessive salivation, and paralysis of the facial muscles, lips, tongue, and larynx. Blood pressure falls, and respiration becomes labored. Drooping eyelids, blurring of vision, convulsions, and headache also occur. Kraits, mambas, taipans, and coral snakes cause less severe reactions at the site of the bite, but abdominal pain is more intense. Severe poisoning is indicated when within one hour there are signs of disturbance to the nervous system—paralysis, mental confusion, or lack of coordination of movements.

First Aid

- As quickly as possible, the victim of any snakebite should be given professional medical care. For many types of envenomization, effective antivenins are now available.
- If possible, try to look at and identify the snake, but do not touch it, even if it is dead.
- Keep the victim prone, calm, and reassured. Any physical activity, including walking, will increase the blood flow and transport the venom more quickly to the rest of the body.

Dangerous Reptilian Creatures

- Immobilize the affected part. If the bite was on the arm, keep it below heart level.
- Carefully wash the area around the bite to remove any surface venom. Remove rings, bracelets, belts, or any tight clothing near the affected area.
- Do not give caffeine or alcoholic drinks.
- For pain do not give aspirin; give paracetamol.
- If you have an extraction kit, such as the Sawyer Extraction Kit, place it over the puncture marks and apply suction for half an hour. Do not use a knife or razor to open the wound and allow it to bleed more freely. You will only spread the poison more quickly.
- If you are *positive* that the snake is a dangerously neurotoxic species, apply a constricting band above the wound or apply pressure over the wound, but only if you are certain of the species and know what you are doing. Do not apply a tourniquet; you may be condemning the victim to the loss of the entire limb.
- Do not attempt the "cut-and-suck" method. You will probably poison yourself. Do not apply cryotherapy, or cold treatment, which was popular 30 to 40 years ago. It does not slow the spread of the venom and often causes irreversible damage to the circulatory system, sometimes requiring amputations.

Treatment

Treatments vary with the species, location of the bite, the degree of envenomization, the overall health of the victim, and so on. The following are general procedures.

Antivenin

In spite of the side effects it may produce, antivenin is the most effective treatment and should be administered as soon as possible. It is most effective within four hours after the bite. It is of less value after 8 hours and of questionable value after 24 hours. Antivenin cannot undo damage already

Appendix I

done. It can only block further effects or keep the present ones from worsening. To reduce unpleasant side effects, antivenin is administered slowly by intravenous injection.

Pain
Meperidine may be given for pain.

Sedation
Anxiety may be relieved by sedatives and tranquilizers.

Blood transfusions
Excessive blood loss may be alleviated by blood transfusions.

Antibiotics
A broad-spectrum antibiotic should be given if the reaction to envenomization is severe.

Tetanus
A tetanus injection should be administered.

Respiratory Failure
The victim may need artificial respiration.

New Treatments

There are two new treatments that are quite controversial. Fasciotomy is a surgical procedure that should be performed only by qualified surgeons. To relieve massive swelling, the doctor cuts through the fascia, the connective tissues that support and separate the muscles, to release the pressure underneath.

The second new treatment is electric shock therapy. Ronald Guderian, an American missionary physician in the Amazonian rain forest of Ecuador, successfully treated 34 Ecuadoran Indians using a crude version of the taser, or police stun gun, a small contraption that uses a 9-volt battery to produce a debilitating electric shock. Exactly why this works is not known, but it is effective. Lives have also been saved by tapping electric power from the outboard motor of a boat.

Dangerous Reptilian Creatures

Antivenin Reaction
Also known as serum sickness, these side effects are most prevalent among people with a history of allergic reactions. There is some kind of reaction to antivenin in about 74 percent of the cases. Mild reactions produce rashes, itching, and a throbbing headache. More serious reactions involve coughing, vomiting, wheezing, and a fall in blood pressure that may lead to unconsciousness.

Treatment for antivenin reactions consists of injections of adrenaline at the first sign of symptoms. Antihistamines may also be effective.

Snakebite Prevention
- If you are going to travel in a remote, infested area, you may want to carry your own antivenin with you. Ask your physician to prescribe a commercially available antivenin for you. Although the new dehydrated serums can be kept at temperatures below 90°F, they should be refrigerated whenever possible and only administered by someone trained in their use.
- You may also want to carry an extraction kit.
- Avoid snake charmers and handlers, even if you are told that their snakes have been defanged.
- If a snake approaches you, FREEZE.
- In snake-infested areas wear heavy, high-top boots and heavy canvas leggings. More than half of all snakebites are on the lower part of the leg.
- At night, carry a strong flashlight to light your way. Stomp around as you walk. A snake might not see you, but it will feel your approach through ground vibrations and scurry away.
- Be careful where you place your hands. Avoid caves and tombs. Do not pick up logs or rocks. Be careful around abandoned buildings. Do not camp near rock, trash, or woodpiles.
- If you must sleep outside, raise your cot at least a foot off the ground.

APPENDIX II:
Bites, Gorings, Maulings, and Shock

One does not have to be lost in the African bush or wandering through the rain forests of South America to be bitten, gored, or mauled by an animal. In the United States, 1 million people per year require hospital treatment because of animal attacks. The primary culprits in these incidents are dogs (man's so-called best friend), but bears, cats, rats, bats, hamsters, coyotes, bulls, raccoons, possums, ferrets, wild pigs, goats, horses, and moose—not to mention nonmammals such as snakes and alligators—are responsible for their share of injuries as well.

The nature of an animal attack will depend upon the animal itself. Many mammals, such as dogs, coyotes, rats, and bats, will use their teeth to bite their victim, which will usually result in lacerations and puncture wounds. If the animal has extremely powerful jaws, like the spotted hyena or pit bull terrier, crushed, fractured, and broken bones may result as well. Other mammals may use their claws to scratch, tear, and maul; the most notorious mauler is the grizzly bear, but a stray cat can inflict a painful mauling as well. And many of the larger hoofed mammals, such as moose, rhinos, elephants, and bulls, use antlers or horns to gore and will also trample a victim. (Elephants have even been known to crush people by kneeling, stepping, or sitting on them.) Deep puncture wounds, crushed and broken bones, and severe internal injuries may result. And the danger does not end when the attack does, for there is a serious risk of infection caused by microorganisms that may be present in the animal's saliva or on its claws, paws, horns, or tusks. Virtually all injuries sustained from an

Appendix II

animal attack require tetanus prophylactic (protection from disease) measures, and the threat of rabies must also be considered. In the event of a serious animal attack, immediate first aid may prove to be the difference between life and death.

For gaping abdominal wounds or profuse bleeding from an extremity:
- Cover the wound with a clean cloth, gauze, or sheet dressing.
- Apply direct pressure to stop the bleeding.
- In the event of a severed artery, apply a tourniquet—a band made from a belt, a tie, or another similar object—above the wound to slow the bleeding.
- Keep the victim prone, warm, and calm.

For a puncture wound in the chest:
- Cover the wound with a clean dressing.
- Wrap and knot a rope, belt, tie, or scarf around the chest to keep the wound closed.
- Keep the victim prone, warm, and calm.

For a puncture wound caused by the bite of a dog or a smaller animal:
- Clean the wound immediately and thoroughly, using antiseptics if they are available.
- Apply a clean dressing.
- Press firmly on the dressing to control bleeding.

Shock

In addition to the injuries that may result from a serious animal attack, the victim may also go into *shock*. Shock is a condition characterized by the failure of the circulatory system to maintain an adequate blood supply to vital organs. Symptoms of shock include hypotension (abnormally low

Dangerous Reptilian Creatures

blood pressure); oliguria (diminished urine output); hyperventilation; cold, clammy, and cyanotic (bluish) skin; a weak and rapid pulse; drowsiness; mental confusion; and anxiety. If left untreated, shock can be fatal.

For initial treatment of shock:
- Use blankets or available clothing to keep the victim warm.
- Keep the victim prone, with the legs slightly elevated to improve circulation.
- Be sure the victim is breathing freely, and be prepared to provide respiratory assistance if necessary. Keep the victim's head turned to one side in case of vomiting.

FURTHER READING

Burton, Dr. Maurice, ed. *Encyclopedia of Animals.* London: Octopus Books, 1972.

Caras, Roger A. *Venomous Animals of the World.* Englewood Cliffs, NJ: Prentice Hall, 1974.

Conant, Roger. *A Field Guide to Reptiles and Amphibians.* Boston: Houghton Mifflin, 1975.

Minton, Sherman A., and Madge Rutherford Minton. *Venomous Reptiles.* New York: Scribners, 1980.

Wood, Gerald L. *Animal Facts and Feats.* New York: Sterling, 1977.

INDEX

Africa, 14, 15, 16, 23, 49, 60, 68, 96
Agkistrodon contortrix, 38. *See also* Copperhead
Agkistrodon piscivorous, 46. *See also* Cottonmouth
Alligator, 48–51
Anaconda, 98
Antarctica, 9
Arizona, 66
Asia, 68, 72, 105
Australia, 50, 108, 109, 110, 112, 113

Barba amarilla, 58. *See also* Fer-de-lance
Bitis gabonica, 62, 63. *See also* Gaboon viper
Black Mamba, 11, 14–17, 117
Blood flukes, 18–21
Boomslang, 22–25
Bothrops asper, 58. *See also* Fer-de-lance
Brazil, 27
Bufo, 90. *See also* Neotropical toads
Bungarus, 82. *See also* Krait
Bushmaster, 26–29, 60

California newt, 101, 102
Caras, Roger A., 15, 52, 116
Central America, 26, 89, 94
Cercariae, 20
Chappell Island, 114
China, 19, 32, 74, 81
Cobra, 30–35, 52, 56, 81, 106, 112, 117
Colombia, 93
Colombian arrow-poison frog, 92
Colorado River, 64
Copperhead, 36–39
Coral snake, 40–43, 116, 117
Cottonmouth, 38, 44–47
Crocodile, 10, 48–51
Crocodylus porosus, 50. *See also* Crocodile
Crotalus adamanteus, 54. *See also* Diamondback rattlesnake
Crotalus atrox, 54. *See also* Diamondback rattlesnake

Dahomey, Africa, 96
Death adder, 112
Dendroaspis Polylepis, 16. *See also* Black Mamba
Dendrobatidae, 92. *See also* Poison frogs
Diamondback rattlesnake, 52–55
Dispholidus typus, 24. *See also* Boomslang
Dracunculiasis, 68, 70, 71
Dracunculus medinensis, 69. *See also* Guinea worm

Ecuador, 119
Edema, 34, 38, 55, 58, 106, 116
Egypt, 19
Elapidae, 16, 32, 110, 117
Electric shock therapy, 119

Fasciotomy, 119
Fer-de-lance, 56–59
Florida, 44, 54

Gaboon viper, 60–63
Gangrene, 46, 47, 63, 74
Georgia, 44
Gila monster, 64–67
Guinea worm, 68–71

Dangerous Reptilian Creatures

Habu, 72–75
Haemadipsidae, 86. *See also* Land leech
Haiti, 97
Heloderma horridum, 66. *See also* Mexican beaded lizard
Heloderma suspectum, 66. *See also* Gila monster
Hyla, 94. *See also* Poison frogs

Iceland, 9
India, 30, 52, 71, 81, 104, 105
Ireland, 9

Japan, 72

King cobra, 33. *See also* Cobra
Kokoi arrow-poison frog, 92–93
Komodo dragon, 76–79
Krait, 80–83, 117

Lachesis mutus, 28. *See also* Bushmaster
Land leech, 84–87
Leptomicrurus, 42. *See also* Coral snake

Madras, India, 81
Martinique, 56
Medina worm, 69. *See also* Guinea worm
Mesopotamia, 19

Mexican beaded lizard, 64, 66
Micruroides, 42. *See also* Coral snake
Micrurus, 42. *See also* Coral snake
Middle East, 68
Mississippi, 45
Mongoose, 56
Myanmar, 74
Mysore, India, 31

Naja, 32. *See also* Cobra
Nematode, 69
Neotropical toad, 88–91
New Guinea, 110
New Zealand, 9
Nigeria, 96
Nile River, 18, 19, 49
North America, 42, 52
Notechis scutatus, 113. *See also* Tiger snake

Oceania, 50
Okinawa, 72, 73, 74
Oregon newt, 102. *See also* Rough-skinned newt
Oxyuranus scutellatus, 110. *See also* Taipan

Phyllobates, 94. *See also* Poison frogs
Pit vipers, 26, 27, 28, 46, 55, 56, 57, 58, 72, 74, 116
Poison frogs, 92–95

Puff adder, 61, 62
Puffer fish, 102
Pythoninae, 98
Python reticulatus, 98. *See also* Reticulated python

Rain forests, 94, 98, 119
Reptiles
  anatomy, 9–10
  early species, 9
  evolution, 9
  habitat, 9
  locomotion, 10
  mating habits, 10
  number of species, 9
Reticulated Python, 96–99
Rough-skinned newt, 100–103
Russell's viper, 104–7, 112
Ryukyu Islands, 72, 73, 74

Schistosomes, 20
Snakebites
  about, 10, 116–120
  envenomization, 10–11, 116–17
  first aid, 117–118
  number of incidents, United States, 10
  prevention, 55, 120
  serum sickness, 120
  treatment, 118–19
Snake charmers, 31, 97, 120

Index

Sonoran Desert, 64
South America, 26, 42, 89, 90, 94, 116
Southeast Asia, 74, 77, 98, 112
South Pacific, 50, 112
Sri Lanka, 85, 106
Syrup of ipecac, 91, 95, 103

Taipan, 108–11, 117
Taiwan, 72, 74
Tanzania, 62, 96
Taricha granulosa, 102. *See also* Rough-skinned newt
Tasmania, 112
Terciopelo, 58. *See also* Fer-de-lance
Tetanus, 46, 58, 119
Texas, 53
Tiger snakes, 112–15, 117
Trematodes, 20
Trimeresurus, 74. *See also* Habu

Triturus, 100

Uganda, 49, 96
United States, 10, 36–37, 38, 40, 43, 52–53, 54, 65, 89, 97
Upper Volta, 71

Varanus komodoensis, 78. *See also* Komodo dragon

West Indies, 56, 89

Missy Allen is a writer and photographer whose work has appeared in *Time*, *Geo*, *Vogue*, *Paris-Match*, *Elle*, and many European publications. Allen holds a master's degree in education from Boston University. Before her marriage to Michel Peissel, she worked for the Harvard School of Public Health and was director of admissions at Harvard's Graduate School of Arts and Sciences.

Michel Peissel is an anthropologist, explorer, inventor, and author. He has studied at the Harvard School of Business, Oxford University, and the Sorbonne. Called "the last true adventurer of the 20th century," Peissel discovered 14 Mayan sites in the eastern Yucatán at the age of 21 and was the youngest member ever elected to the New York Explorers Club. He is also one of the world's foremost experts on the Himalayas, where he has led 14 major expeditions. Peissel has written 14 books, which have been published in 83 editions in 15 countries.

When not found in their fisherman's house in Cadaqués, Spain, with their two young children, Peissel and Allen can be found trekking across the Himalayas or traveling in Central America.

ACKNOWLEDGMENTS

The authors would like to thank Lisa Bateman for her editorial assistance; Brian Rankin for his careful typing; Carla Maristany for her graphic designs; and Linnie Greason, Heather Moulton, and Luis Abiega for so kindly allowing their lives to be infiltrated by these creepy crawlies and ferocious fauna.

CREDITS

All the original watercolor illustrations are by Michel Peissel. The geographic distribution maps are by Diana Blume.